The Beautiful List

THE BEAUTIFUL LIST

a novel

Christine Virgin

NEW YORK

LONDON • NASHVILLE • MELBOURNE • VANCOUVER

THE BEAUTIFUL LIST

a novel

Published in New York, New York, by Morgan James Publishing. Morgan James is a trademark of Morgan James, LLC. www.MorganJamesPublishing.com

Publisher's Note: This novel is a work of fiction. Names, characters, places, and incidents are either products of the author's imagination or used fictitiously. All characters are fictional, and any similarity to people living or dead is purely coincidental.

Scriptures taken from the Holy Bible, New International Version®, NIV®. Copyright © 1973, 1978, 1984, 2011 by Biblica, Inc.™ Used by permission of Zondervan. All rights reserved worldwide. www.zondervan.com The "NIV" and "New International Version" are trademarks registered in the United States Patent and Trademark Office by Biblica, Inc.™

Proudly distributed by Ingram Publisher Services.

Morgan James BOGO™

A **FREE** ebook edition is available for you or a friend with the purchase of this print book.

CLEARLY SIGN YOUR NAME ABOVE

Instructions to claim your free ebook edition:
1. Visit MorganJamesBOGO.com
2. Sign your name CLEARLY in the space above
3. Complete the form and submit a photo of this entire page
4. You or your friend can download the ebook to your preferred device

ISBN 9781631958649 paperback
ISBN 9781631958656 ebook
Library of Congress Control Number:
2021952840

Cover Design by:
Megan Dillon
megan@creativeninjadesigns.com

Interior Design by:
Chris Treccani
www.3dogcreative.net

Morgan James PUBLISHING **Builds** with... **Habitat for Humanity®** Peninsula and Greater Williamsburg

Morgan James is a proud partner of Habitat for Humanity Peninsula and Greater Williamsburg. Partners in building since 2006.

Get involved today! Visit MorganJamesPublishing.com/giving-back

For my girls, Brooke and Eliza—may you know the depths of your beauty—and my boys, Zach and Ethan—may you honor, love, and respect girls and women for the marvelous creations they are.

Prologue

Twelve-and-a-half years ago

"What do we have?" the ER doctor asked calmly as he pulled his mask over his nose and mouth, the last step in preparing himself for emergency surgery.

"Two stab wounds: one to the chest, causing the collapsed lung, and the one on the cheek," the nurse explained as she monitored several machines. A surgical tech was busily prepping tools, and an anesthesiologist quietly readied her patient's IV bags.

"Have you contacted the plastic surgeon on call?"

"It's Dr. Reynolds. He's coming."

Dr. Brody looked down at his patient.

"Can you hear me?"

The woman's eyelids created slits through which you could only see the whites of her eyes, but she was still conscious. Barely. She mumbled something incoherent.

"We're going to take care of you. You're going to be okay," he said.

Just then, the OR doors opened, and one of the top plastic surgeons in the Washington, DC, metro area walked in.

"Dr. Reynolds, when I'm finished with her lung, she's all yours."

"What happened, do we know?" Dr. Reynolds asked as he glanced at the woman's face and chest.

"All the police said was that she was assaulted," the nurse responded, still prepping the patient and room.

As Dr. Reynolds examined her further, he thought the woman looked familiar.

"What's the patient's name?"

"Nadia Orlov," the nurse responded after examining a chart.

"I think I know her from somewhere. I'm going to call Elenore while you work on her lung." Dr. Brody shrugged, wondering why his colleague wouldn't simply wait to call his wife.

The anesthesiologist covered Nadia's face with a mask that would deliver the drugs to put her under.

"Do your best, and I'll do mine. Poor woman," Dr. Reynolds muttered as he patted Dr. Brody on the shoulder before crashing back through the double doors. "What a tragedy for such a beautiful face."

Chapter 1:
RACHEL, PLAIN AND LARGE

"What Makes You Beautiful"

—ONE DIRECTION

Imperfection is beauty.

—MARILYN MONROE

Today

"Beautiful, be ready when they call our number," he says.

It's the third time I've heard him call her beautiful in just a few minutes.

I study them both. I am very good at reading people, and one thing is clear: She believes him. This family of five, like ours, is waiting to board the same plane as us. We're heading home from spring break in Florida. The mom tells us this girl is seven years old. That's four or five years younger than I am, depending on when she was born. I keep staring at her as my own mom interrupts my thoughts.

"Sweetie, don't sit down. Walk around with me. We'll be sitting for the next three hours."

I know my mom well enough to know she is trying to burn calories. As I pace, trying to keep up with her, I can't help but stare. The first thing I think anyone would notice about this girl is that she is big in every way for a seven-year-old: She is tall and round. Her older brother and sister don't look nearly as big for their ages (which their mom said are ten and twelve). Her parents are both average-sized. The girl's head might be the biggest part of her proportionately, and a close second are her frizzy, dark, and out-of-control curls. She is—to me, anyway—plain and interesting looking. Imagine Hagrid from *Harry Potter* had a baby with Drizella, the dark-haired sister from *Cinderella*.

The thing is, I'm plain too. Have you heard of *Sarah, Plain and Tall*? I've never read it and don't know what it's about, but I sometimes think it would be my title if I were a book, only Sarah would be spelled with an *e*, and I'd be "Serah, Plain and Taller than Average." And this girl? Her dad would call her "Beautiful, Plain and Beautiful," which seems completely bizarro to me.

As I continue staring, then looking away so she doesn't catch me staring, we accidentally make eye contact. I'm embarrassed but don't want to be rude, so I give her a mouth-closed-not-really-real smile, and she returns my attempt at being nice with a full-faced grin. Maybe she's more like a *Pollyanna* than a *Sarah, Plain and Tall.*

Now she's walking toward me, totally misjudging my fake smile. I give up on keeping pace with my mom and stop, seeing no way out of a confrontation with Miss Happy Pants.

"What's *your* name?" the girl asks me sweetly.

"I'm Seraphina, but I go by Serah," I respond while looking everywhere but at her, trying to show her how bored I am.

"I'm Rachel, and I'm just like you!"

At this, I turn around to look behind me, searching for the person she must be talking to back there. Then I feel a twinge of guilt, thinking that is ruder than I want to be.

"I have an older brother, then a sister, and then I'm the youngest. Isn't that the same in your family? Your brother looks older than your sister."

"Oh, yeah," I manage to get out. I'm grateful that's what she meant and not that she thought we looked alike. There's another twinge of guilt.

"I like your name; it's really cool," she continues.

"Thanks," I murmur. I wonder if anyone has noticed us. Why would that matter? Somehow, it seems to. But I'm bored anyway and have nothing better to do than speed walk with my mom. Rachel either doesn't seem to notice my indifference, or she doesn't care, though, 'cause she keeps talking.

"Do you know what it means?"

"What *what* means?"

"Your name!"

This pulls me in. One of my hobbies is to look up the meaning of people's names. I could talk about names *all day*.

"That's actually a funny story," I say. "My mom, who's over there but heading back toward us, is Italian, and she wanted to give us all Italian names. My brother over there is Alessandro, and my sister is Vittoria. When I looked up my name, though, it turns out it's Hebrew," I confess. Then in a whisper: "I haven't had the heart to tell my mom yet, though."

At this, Rachel starts giggling, and it turns into a very infectious laugh with knee-slapping. This is actually adorable.

"THAT IS HILARIOUS!" she bellows. Then, coming close and cupping her hand around her mouth like something super-secret and important is about to be whispered, she asks, "So what does your mom think your name means in Italian?"

"Well, she got the spelling wrong, is all," I whisper back. "The Italian spelling for Serafina is S-E-R-A-F-I-N-A. The spelling with *ph*, like my name, is Hebrew. They both come from *seraphim*, meaning 'fiery-winged.'"

Alessandro means "defender of mankind," and Vittoria means "victory." I think my parents were warriors in another life or something. I'm debating whether to say all this out loud, but Rachel again breaks the silence before I get the chance.

"That's amazing!" she gushes. "I mean, soooooooooo cool." It seems very obvious that she has no idea what fiery-winged means. "My mom told me my name is also Hebrew, and it means 'beautiful.'"

Of course that's her name. At this, she takes a twirl as if to reveal her full glory to me. Maybe her dad uses Rachel and the word beautiful interchangeably. That would make a little more sense. I make a mental note to look up the name Rachel for alternate meanings. While *I* don't think her name fits, which brings on another twinge of guilt, it's clear that *she* thinks it does. I can tell because she seems light and confident. If you ask me, her dad constantly calling her beautiful is over the top, making me wonder if he is trying to make up for something (like her big head). Or maybe he just really wants her to hear it.

I can't quite pinpoint why I find this girl to be both endearing and annoying at the same time. Honestly, I would be bothered if my dad called me beautiful constantly. And yet, I think to myself that she has made me aware of something I didn't realize I was bothered by until now. It couldn't hurt to hear it *sometimes*.

My thoughts are interrupted by the Delta lady behind the counter, who booms over the PA system, "We are now preboarding Delta flight 2961 to Washington-Reagan at Gate 38. We'd like to welcome any passengers needing assistance or active-duty military personnel with ID to begin boarding."

At this news, Rachel's mom waves her over to where her family is standing. She turns to me.

"I have to go, but it was really nice to meet you." At that, she crosses one foot over the other and does a dance-like 180-degree pivot, throws her head back over her shoulder, cocks it to the side with glee, and waves as she energetically bounces off. "Bye, Seraphina. Maybe I'll see you in Washington, DC!"

As I am left in her wake, I wonder: What does *she* have that I *don't* have? What's wrong with me? I'm a twelve-year-old who is feeling jealous of this seven-year-old—"Rachel, Plain and Large," to be exact, now that I know her name. That sounds so mean. I'm not trying to be, but facts are facts. But somehow, she also lives up to her name.

I've always thought "fiery-winged" is a good name for me. I'm pretty feisty, curious, and bold, and I've always appreciated having these qualities. I tell myself this is just a moment, and it will soon be history. Rachel's gone, and I'm never going to see her again.

We board a few minutes later, and while we're tucking our carry-on luggage under seats and in overhead bins to settle in, I hear my parents talking about Rachel.

"Did you see the girl who was talking to Serah?" my mom asks my dad.

"Yes, and if she were my daughter, I'd have her tested to make sure she doesn't have pathologic macrocephaly."

"I thought the same thing when I saw her. Poor girl," my mom says sympathetically. They are constantly having conversations like this about people.

As they continue to discuss the possible medical reasons for her large head—which I'm assuming is what they're talking about—and what could be done about it, I can't get her out of my mind.

Once our row is situated, I pull out my binder from my backpack and grab a sheet of notebook paper and my favorite pen with the feather on the end. I shove the huge sack back under the seat in front of me and pull down my tray table. Carefully, I fold the sheet in half lengthwise and then write at the top: "BEAUTIFUL." Then I label the column on the left "Things That Are" and the column on the right "Things That Are *Definitely* Not." I add Rachel's name in the first line on the left and stare at it for a bit, knowing that's where it goes. Beneath her name, I add my mom, my sister, and my Siamese cat, Sophia Loren. I add my BFF, Courtney. Then I try to think of other things that I know are beautiful as I look out the airplane window and see the final bags getting loaded underneath me.

I add sunrises, sunsets, flowers, scoring goals, A-pluses, and babies. To the right column, I add boys, body odor, war, famine, climate change, and poop.

It's time to put up my tray table for takeoff. Once we're in the air, I peer out the window again at the beautiful sky. When I look back down at my list, I realize what's missing from it.

This is how it all starts.

Chapter 2:
HOT OR NOT?

Like I said, I'm Seraphina—Seraphina Isabella Reynolds, to be exact. Isabella is also Italian, sort of a derivative of Elizabeth, which means "God is my oath." But we're not really religious; we go to Mass on Christmas and Easter, which someone told me means we're "Chreaster Christians." I think that's a funny word for it. I also think my parents just liked the name Isabella.

You already know my mom, Elenore Reynolds, is Italian. Not, like, born and raised there, but her parents emigrated to the US before they had her. This explains how she has no idea how to spell in Italian. She can speak it and understand it when people speak to her, but she can't read or write it. Elenore means "light," and, for the most part, I think it fits. Everywhere I go, people tell me how nice she is. 😊

And my dad, William, is Scottish. His name means "resolute protector." I guess in a way it fits because he is very protective of us, especially my sister and me. He was born in Scotland, so he has this really cool accent. But he went to medical school here and then stayed for his residency. My mom said that because we all got a Scottish last name, it only made sense that we would get Italian first names.

I'm twelve years old, and for the first time in my life, I feel awkward, even insecure. Like, all the time. It started sometime around age ten or eleven and hasn't gone away. I can forget about it a lot of the time, but it always comes back. Maybe it's like having your period—it goes away, but you know it's just a matter of time before you have it again. I feel *most* awkward in a bathing suit. I never used to think much about what I was wearing until this year. I'm *technically* in middle school, but my school divides lower and middle school between sixth and seventh grades, which means I get an extra year of elementary school. 😊 (I like eye-rolling.)

Not only am I thinking more about what I'm wearing but also about how it looks and what other people will think or say about it. I've noticed that some other girls care a *lot* about how their outfits look, where they're bought, and whether they have a crocodile, a whale, or some other logo on them. Personally, I think having a pink whale on

9

your plain white shirt means that now your outfit has to coordinate with that pink whale, and your shirt is no longer plain. But what do I know?

Another reason bathing suits now seem cringey is that I've become increasingly aware of my non-developing yet aching breasts. (It seems entirely unfair that they should pulse and hurt, especially if they get bumped.) In fourth grade, there was one girl in school who had started sprouting *actual* breasts: Jordan Fleming. This was entirely fine with me because, in fourth grade, I didn't want the attention of being the first to do anything other than solving a math problem or scoring a soccer goal. Then last year, a few more started growing them. And now many girls are beginning to "bloom" (ew, that's what our health teacher called it), and I haven't started. I wear a training bra or a camisole underneath my shirts—especially white ones—because it would seem inappropriate for my breasts to be noticeable, even if they aren't growing. This is another reason why I don't want symbols or logos of any kind on the chest area of my clothes. It's like adding a billboard on them that's shouting, "Stare at me until you figure out there's nothing here!"

Mandy King, probably the most popular girl in school, likes to talk about *everyone*. Just before spring break, while we were all changing for PE, she asked, "Serah, like, um, why do you wear a bra when you don't, like, need one?" while her minions, Regina and Gretchen, snickered next to her. Ignoring the fact that she, too, hasn't "bloomed" and *also* wears a bra, I wanted to say in her same nasty voice, "For the same reason, like, that you carry a pad around." And while that would have been a really good burn, it would only have made me a bigger target. So, instead, I tried humor.

"It's a training bra," I said. "I'm training them to grow!" And then I laughed really hard—a little forced, I'll admit—along with Jessica and Liv, who could hear the conversation and had come over to support me.

I've found that the best way to deal with Mandy is by laughing about her stupid comments. Courtney, my BFF, and I started calling her Veruca Salt behind her back a couple years ago after reading about the bratty, entitled character in *Charlie and the Chocolate Factory*.

Of course, between my own awareness that breasts all around me are growing and mine should start any day, my bathing suit seems like an advertisement of what's happening in that area. Every time I wore one in Florida, I wondered whether anyone was looking at me and noticing my lack of breasts like Mandy apparently does.

I have light brown hair and hazel eyes, which I think must be what happens when you blend a fair-skinned Scottish dad with a tan Italian mom. My left eye is all hazel; my right eye is all hazel except for one section that is dark brown, which my parents have told me is called a sectoral heterochromia. And I love this about myself.

I realize I need to add my eyes to my list of things that are beautiful. Before heading downstairs, I rummage through my desk to the secret drawer where I keep private stuff, pull out the sheet of notebook paper that I carefully tucked in there as soon as we walked in the door from our trip, and I add my eyes to the left column. At least I can say that part of me belongs on the Beautiful List.

A week has gone by since that flight when I met Rachel, and I've been wondering a lot about appearances. And while I never really thought about it much before, my own appearance is on my mind. *What do I look like to strangers?* I wonder. I mean, everyone is different and unique, right?

Part of me feels I must be strange, ungrateful, or even selfish for even having these questions and feelings. It is very clear to me that I have a great life. There's a girl in my grade, Tina, who has to walk with these custom crutches because her legs didn't develop the way they were supposed to. Just doing normal things that almost everyone can do is a challenge for her.

Courtney's dad travels most of the week every week because he's a rock star consultant, and she has told me many times how much she wishes he were around. It makes my dad's trips to the hospital here and there seem like no biggie. I have parents who love each other and love us. We have a nice house, fancy cars, and are never in need. Being the baby, I can admit that I get away with a lot of things my brother and sister would not have gotten away with when they were my age, like lying about having a stomachache to get a lollipop (and having it work) and putting my mom's makeup on our cat without getting in trouble.

To people on the outside, I'm sure my life looks amazing, maybe even jealous-worthy. I would be lying if I didn't say that sometimes it feels nice to imagine others being jealous of me. I am, after all, heading downstairs to my indoor swimming pool in Potomac, Maryland, in *April*. (Holla!) But Rachel is on my mind, and I'm still feeling jealous of her. Why? I don't know who said it, but things aren't always what they seem. From the outside, my life is Insta-worthy and eye-catching and beautiful, like a crowned hairstreak butterfly. Or, like food, I would look like a tasty tiramisu. From the inside, I don't feel so special. I feel plain and blah. Like panna cotta, which is like a Jell-o made of pudding. It's nearly impossible to make panna cotta look pretty. Or like a solid brown moth. Maybe with a speck of color because of my eyes. I can't wait to go to Courtney's later. She always has a way of making me feel better.

◎ ❋ ◎

People who know me tell me I'm pretty grown up. They also tell me I'm smart. The more people say the same thing about you over and over, the more you believe it. My parents have also made me take some test that's supposed to prove that someone is wicked smart. After I took the test, my parents said I could join some smart people's organization. I told them I wasn't interested.

I started reading at a really young age, and because of that, I've been teaching myself all sorts of grown-up things since I was five or six years old. I love *National Geographic* magazine and have a subscription. In my spare time, I read it cover to cover for fun. I'm also mature for my age because Alessandro and Vittoria teach me things, sometimes without knowing it. Alessandro just turned seventeen, and Vittoria is fourteen. Between them and my library, I know a lot (if I do say so myself).

Speaking of Alessandro, my brother's friends like to hang out at our house in our pool and play pool—no joke—on an inflatable pool table. Today my sister is prancing around in a bikini in front of them, which I watch out of the corner of my eye, trying not to LOL.

It is obvious to me that there is some agreement that means Vittoria is off-limits to them. I'm not sure if my brother ever said something to his friends to make it clear they aren't allowed to crush on or date my sister. (And she's technically not allowed to date yet, anyway, but that hasn't stopped her from having secret boyfriends.) Or maybe there is some unspoken guy rule that doesn't even have to be said: Your friends' sisters are not dateable. Plus, they're in high school, and she's still in middle school. Vittoria seems to be ignorant about all of this though. She is doing her best to draw their attention away from their game of pool by making waves, pretending they're an accident, giggling, and hiding underwater. Honestly, I wonder how she could be so silly. For a moment, I wonder if she is actually stupid or if she is playing stupid. I've seen her and her friends *play* dumb in front of my brother's friends before, which I don't understand at all. I'd much rather be smart and plain than dumb and pretty. At least most of the time.

And speaking of Vittoria, I imagine the way these guys ignore her is strange for her. Most guys stare at my sister. I've been to the mall shopping with her exactly three times, and every time, I've noticed guys noticing her. She is curvy and looks like an Italian model minus the height, just like my mom. My brother looks more like my dad and has lighter coloring. He and his friends either don't believe we can hear the words coming out of their mouths, or they don't care if we do.

"I would hook up with Megan Carlyle," one of my brother's buddies, Justin, says while sinking a striped pool ball into a corner pocket. I halfheartedly read my *National Geographic*, pretending to mind my own business. "She's totally hot."

"Yeah, me too," Ryan chimes in. "But what about Becca? I really want to ask her to prom."

"Becca Bromwell or Bekah Woods?" Justin asks.

"Bromwell," Ryan says as if he's offended Justin didn't think that was obvious.

"Mmm, I don't know. She's not that hot, so maybe you have a chance," he replies with a laugh.

"HEY, watch it!" Ryan jokes back while he jumps on Justin, dunking him underwater. The pool balls roll around from the waves, messing up their game.

"Bekah Woods is hot for sure," Justin offers as he resurfaces.

"Alessandro, who's hotter?" Ryan asks my brother as if his opinion on this will be the tie-breaking vote on the subject. I watch to see my brother's response. He's busy re-racking the pool balls.

"I'd say Becca Bromwell," Alessandro finally offers up. "But they're both hot. If either of them gave me the time of day, I'd be into her."

In my head, I imagine these two girls standing on a stage in bikinis with sashes hanging across their shoulders while they wave to an audience. Instead of the sashes saying "Miss Virginia" or "Miss Maryland," like in a beauty pageant, the sashes simply say "Hot or not?" Then I imagine the girls taking off their sashes, walking over to Justin and Ryan at the judges' tables, draping the sashes over these jocks' heads, and yelling, "NOT!" while they walk away together, shaking their heads.

As I turn back to the cover story about the impacts of global warming and krill fishing on Antarctica's leopard seals, I ponder the evaluation system behind "hot" or "not." I decide I'll ask my brother about it later. He will be a really good source for my secret research 'cause he's a guy. I imagine a leopard seal beauty pageant, where the animals are presented to be sold to the highest bidder. They're wearing cute pink sashes that define them as "Miss Iceberg," "Miss Deep Sea Diver," and such. How different the measure of outer beauty between seals and girls, since seals are more desirable with more blubber. I think about how beautiful leopard seals are and decide I'll add them to my Beautiful List when I get upstairs.

I return to reality, where my brother and his friends are now talking about their next baseball game. I check my iPod to find a good song and notice it's almost four o'clock. I've got to get ready for my sleepover at Courtney's! As I walk past the pool of teenage boys, I can't help but wonder if any of them look at my backside in my bathing suit. Or if any of them noticed my non-existent chest. Then I think how gross that would be. And I decide that next time, I'll wrap my towel around myself before walking by.

◉ ❋ ◉

Once in my room, I remove my suit and examine my body in the mirror. I stare at the "bug bites" on my chest. I wonder when they will start to grow, how quickly it will happen, and how big they'll get. Vittoria wears a size 32C bra, but based on research I did online, sisters don't necessarily grow up to have similar-sized breasts. My mom's side of the family is what I've heard her call "well-endowed," but my dad's mom and sister are both pretty small chested. I sigh. My gaze goes down to my legs. My long, skinny, shapeless legs. They've been called noodles, threads, twigs, and sticks. Are they beautiful? Am I? Sophia Loren slinks around my ankles as if to say, "Yes." I don't think I'm "hot," but I don't think I'm "not." When I was little, I was "cute as a button," which graduated into "cute." But it kind of feels like cute is a consolation prize. Like runner-up in a beauty pageant.

Chapter 3:
LEG SWAP

"Unpretty"

—TLC

*Women are beautiful, every single one of us.
It is one of the glorious ways that we bear the
image of God. But few of us believe we are
beautiful, and fewer still are comfortable with it.*

—STASI ELDREDGE, *CAPTIVATING*

"Seraphina, it's time to gooooooooo!" I hear my mom call from downstairs. I run down to find her in her Puma sneakers, matching Athleta workout gear, high ponytail, and makeup. I catch a glimpse of *Project Runway* on the kitchen TV.

"Are you heading to the gym, Mom?"

Before she turns to me, she mutters under her breath, "That woman needs rhinoplasty." Once she makes eye contact, her mind focuses. "Yes, after I drop you off. Are you ready to—" She stops mid-sentence, looking me up-and-down. "Seraphina, WHAT are you *wearing*?"

"Clothes?"

"Sweetie, I am going to the gym to exercise, but that doesn't mean I dress like a homeless person who's begging on the street corner. Your pants have holes in them, and that shirt has stains everywhere." This statement is cause for flailing arms. I have been told by my dad that this is the Italian in her.

"Mom, I'm only going to Courtney's. We're just going to be hanging out. Don't worry; if we go anywhere, I have a change of clothes, so I won't *embarrass* you if I see any of your country club friends."

My mom takes a deep breath, one of those where she looks up at the ceiling as she slowly exhales to buy herself time to think. Some might call it an eye roll, and maybe it is—and maybe it's where I get it from. "I just thought you'd care about being a bit more presentable, that's all. Let's go."

We get in the car, and I think about my family: my mom, the Italian bombshell; my brother, the athlete; my sister, Miss Popular and junior bombshell; and my dad, the plastic surgeon. He is highly respected and known for being a top-notch doctor. When you walk into his office, the sign says, "Realize your full potential." I never really thought about his job much before because I know people generally feel better after they go to him. He has told me countless stories about helping patients who have a real need for surgical reconstruction: breast cancer survivors, accident victims, and even children born with deformities—cases he does for free. But he also performs elective surgeries on people who want to change something about how they look. Now that I think about it, his slogan is based on the idea that something about you is wrong and should be fixed—or at the very least, could be better. He and my mom met twenty years ago when she was one of his *elective* patients. Actually, it was for a rhinoplasty—the fancy word for a nose job. She has worked with him ever since.

"Did you see that skirt I bought you and laid out on your bed?" My mom's question snaps me out of my train of thought.

"Yep," I say, grateful that we're almost to Courtney's.

"Well, I thought maybe you'd want to wear it," she confesses.

"Thanks for getting it for me, but it's not really my style. I'm not really into pink poodles anymore," I respond.

"Oh," she says, but in that way moms say "oh" that really means "ouch." It makes you want to erase what you just said because you *never* want to *unintentionally* make your mom feel bad. Doing it on purpose is one thing. Doing it accidentally is another.

"I can probably wear it soon," I offer. *What am I saying*? I don't really want to wear that.

"Okay," she says. "I was surprised you weren't wearing the skirt, and I think I overreacted. I'm sorry that I made a big deal about your outfit. I have to accept that you're growing up, and I need to let you make your own choices.

But when I saw it, I thought it would be really cute on you. It falls right beneath the knee, which would help make your legs look curvier. You definitely inherited the 'Reynolds legs.'" She delivers that last part with air quotes.

"Thanks, Mom," I say sarcastically. I suddenly can't wait to get to Courtney's. My mind wanders to "Rachel, Plain and Large and Beautiful." I wonder what my parents would suggest should be done about her large head. They often mention some sort of plastic surgery procedure while watching TV. If my mom and dad are together in a room, they will discuss how they could make someone look better by doing this or that to them. It's kind of weird.

"Mom, what's ma-cro-sef-ly?"

"Macrocephaly? That's a medical term for a large head."

"When we flew home from Florida, there was that girl in the airport. Do you remember her? Were you worried about her?"

"Oh, now I get it. Um, no, not *really*. Lots of people have completely benign large heads. But sometimes, a large head indicates a medical problem, such as fluid in the brain or an enlarged brain, for example."

Rachel didn't seem to me like anything was wrong with her brain. She also didn't seem aware of her large head. And neither did her family. In fact, her family thought she was *beautiful*.

Luckily, we pull into Courtney's driveway, and I forget about Rachel and poodle skirts and fancy medical words about big heads, at least for a little while.

◦ ✳ ◦

My BFF, Courtney, and I go wayyyy back. The name Courtney comes from French and means two *very* different things. One is "of the court," as in royalty, and the other is "short nose," which I think is funny. Obviously, Courtney's name means she is like royalty, at least to me, anyway. Courtney is an only child, so I love staying at her place because I don't have to deal with my brother or sister complaining that we're bugging them.

Courtney is funny, playful, kind, and caring. When we disagree, we find a way to work it out. I think we both knew it was meant to be when, in kindergarten, we invented a new tunnel system in the sandbox together that changed every kid's playground life forever.

Today, though, despite my initial excitement, she can tell I'm deep in thought and not my usual self.

"What's up, Serah?"

I look her in the eyes the way you can only do with someone you completely trust. It just comes out.

"Do you ever feel like something's wrong with you?" I ask.

"Um, all the TIME!" she blurts, LOLing. "I *know* something's wrong with me. My mom says I'm too silly about half of the time."

"No, seriously, Court," I say.

"Like, *actually* something wrong?"

22

"Well, like, do you ever feel like maybe you don't fit in 'cause you're not enough? Or that you're a big disappointment, even though no one has said you are?"

"Whoa, are you okay? It sounds like we need ice cream." And without waiting for me to respond, she heads toward the kitchen, so I follow her, wondering if this is worth talking about at all. At the end of the hall, she turns around and holds her finger to her mouth to indicate I should be quiet while she checks to see if the coast is clear. She tiptoes out into the kitchen and motions that it's safe. Her mom must be in her room.

"Alright, what's going on?" she whispers as she scoops a huge spoonful of cookies and cream into a large Hello Kitty bowl as quickly as she can. It seems childish like I've outgrown Hello Kitty, though I don't know when.

"I am not sure I even know how to put it into words, Court. We don't have to talk about this. I've just been thinking about some things."

"Okay, but, like, what?" she pushes, still whispering. She grabs two spoons and motions for us to start tiptoeing back to her room with our treat.

"So, Court, you've been to my house like a million times. What do you think of my family?" I ask as we settle onto her bed, spoons ready to dig in.

"Well, I think your dad is busy a lot, but it's obvious he is proud of you. Your mom is super nice when she is around. They both work hard, just like you," she rattles off. After pausing to down a few bites, she continues.

"Your brother and sister don't seem all that bad, and to be honest, I would give anything to have a brother or a sister, even though I like being an only child." She bores into my eyes with her gaze. "And I would obviously love it if it weren't just my mom and me so much of the time. It can be lonely."

"I know, Court," I whisper. I look away in the distance. *What's wrong with me?* I wonder. Courtney has dealt with so much, and *I'm* the one complaining to *her*.

"Is that what you meant?" she asks.

"Sort of. If it makes you feel any better, even though I'm pretty much never alone at home, I get lonely too."

We sit in silence together for a moment, just eating ice cream.

"I've decided to do a secret research project," I confide to her. "I want to understand and define beauty. I even made a chart to sort it out. But you can't tell ANYONE." I explain the Beautiful List to her, why I made it, and share all about Rachel.

"This girl kind of sounds like a rock star," Courtney says. "But I think you and I were both like her at her age, no? We used to dress up in fancy dresses and princess costumes and twirl and dance as we listened to T. Swift. Don't you remember?"

"I guess I didn't think of that," I respond, thinking. After a pause, I say, "But she was beyond the normal confidence and 'sparkle' of a seven year old. It's like she knew she was totally loved, especially by her dad, so she had this brave confidence that burst out of her like an unstoppable force."

"Yeah, but don't you think we had that at her age?" Courtney asks.

"Not like hers. Which is *why* I made the list."

"What's it for, though? Why make a list at all? What are you going to do once you've defined beauty? And you're the queen of Webster's. What did the dictionary say?"

"*Of course* I looked it up," I say sarcastically. "Then I added the definition to the top of the list. It basically means 'exciting aesthetic pleasure, generally pleasing or excellent.'"

"Okay, so are you done with it?"

"Hardly."

"You're going to have to help me out," Courtney voices like a robot, adding arm movements. "Seriously, girl, what else is there? What's the point?"

"I need to get to the bottom of whether I'm beautiful or not," I say sheepishly, looking down.

"*Of course* you're beautiful!" she yells in disbelief as she squeezes loads of contraband chocolate syrup on our melting ice cream because she's no longer paying attention. I guess it was her turn to be loud.

"Great! I'm glad to hear it. How do you *know* that?" I counter while tipping the bottle back over for her before she turns our ice cream into mostly chocolate syrup.

"'Cause I just know."

"Well, I don't think I am."

"Serah, you're one of the smartest and nicest people I've ever met, and both of those things are definitely beautiful. Your eyes are really pretty, especially that one brown section that you don't notice until you're up close. I love giggling with you, hanging out with you, learning from you—all of that is beautiful."

Now, do you see why she's my BFF?

"Now you do me," she laughs.

I pretend I have a microphone and put on my best newscaster voice. "Well, Courtney, I'd have to say your smile, your kindness, your sense of humor, and your care for those you love are certainly beautiful."

"You forgot to mention my brains," she spits out while swallowing ice cream, so a bit of Oreo lands on my shirt, which she immediately reaches to grab and put back in her mouth. Now, I'm even more grateful I stayed in comfy clothes and didn't listen to my mom about being *presentable*.

"Well, you didn't let me finish!" I snap back. Throat clear. "You are quick-witted, which is a high form of intelligence. Maybe one of the highest," I add with a nod and a smile. "And, Court, I am not sure I've ever mentioned it, but you have killer legs."

"What?!" she squeaks in disbelief. "Come here, NOW—I want to show you something," she says seriously.

She leads me over to her desk, where she has a corkboard full of photos and other mementos, and points at a picture she printed from her iPod of her, Diana, Katie, Liv, and me. Basically, our best friends from soccer.

26

"What do you see when you look at this picture?" she asks.

"Um, a group of sweaty girls after a game?"

"Does anything else stand out to you?" she asks. "What else do you notice?"

"The fact that I'm the only one without any boobs?" I offer.

"Ha! Nooo."

"You're the only African American?"

"Well, that's true and also noticeable but not what I'm thinking of."

I study the picture a little longer. "I give up," I shrug. "But if you're about to dis your legs, you'd better check yourself."

"Compare all of our legs to each other. I have the fattest legs."

I look at her, then at the picture, and back at her as if she's suddenly grown a third arm out of the top of her head.

"You mean you have the most *athletic* and *shapely* legs?"

"Maybe that's how you see them, but what I see when I look at my calves is that they're big," Courtney says.

I'm *so* confused. When did muscle become fat?

"At least Veruca doesn't ask you if you eat every day at lunch while you're clearly chomping down a sandwich." I change my voice to a high-pitched, nasal one. 'Twiggyphina, is this, like, your only, like, meal today?'" I roll my eyes. "My legs are skinny, and for some reason, people

27

have begun to point this out to me as if it were news I need to know—*including* my own mother."

Not only did I have no idea that Courtney didn't like her legs, but I couldn't imagine her ever thinking about them as anything but amazing. I would love to trade legs—and breasts—with her. She reads my mind.

"So I'd rather have *your* legs, and you'd rather have *mine*, huh?"

"In a heartbeat," I say. Another awkward silence.

"So are my legs on your Beautiful List?" Courtney questions and again breaks the tension and silence.

"Not just your legs, Court. You are on the list," I say.

"Interesting," she slowly lets out as she scoops the now-liquid ice cream from the bottom of the bowl. "Who or what else is on it?"

"Not much," I admit. "Boy smell, farts, and poop are *obviously* on the NOT-Beautiful List."

"So obvi."

I pause for effect. "You're one of the first things I put on the list, Courtney."

At this, she smiles.

"And your own name?"

"I didn't put it on there."

"It belongs on there," she smiles at me encouragingly but sounds serious. I'm not so sure, and my silence says what I'm thinking. She sighs.

"So then, how about we finish our ice cream before my mom calls us to dinner?" Courtney suggests.

"Sure, but then you have to tell me about your spring break because I still haven't heard the whole story."

⊙ ❋ ⊙

When I leave Courtney's the next morning after lots more fun and plenty of giggles, I think about what I now know about my best friend that I didn't know before and vice versa.

She's self-conscious too. Courtney, of all people. How could she not like her legs? Or not see how beautiful she is?

Is this normal? I know just where I'm going next to find out.

Chapter 4:

CUTE ENOUGH

"True Colors"

—ANNA KENDRICK AND JUSTIN TIMBERLAKE

I am fearfully and wonderfully made.

—PSALM 139:14

"This is totally normal, Seraphina," Mrs. Caldwell says.

I'm sitting in her office the very next day, doing what I do best: questioning. Besides, I'm pretty sure it's her job to listen to me. At school, you have to listen to your teachers and the principal and staff, but the guidance counselors have to listen to you, right? I kind of like this arrangement.

When I started going to this school in kindergarten, I was assigned to Nadia Caldwell. I like her; her name means "hope." The way they do it, you stick with the same counselor through twelfth grade if you stay here, so they really get to know you if you let them. It's one of the things I really like about being in a private, Christian-based school where they don't force you to take a religion class, just teach kindness and the Golden Rule. While I haven't spent a lot of time with Mrs. Caldwell, I think she is one of the nicest people I've ever met, and she has always seemed to take an interest in me, maybe more than other kids. I've come to trust this woman, and I know she will be honest.

"What's normal?" I ask.

"All of it!" she assures me. "The questioning, the noticing, the wondering. There are so many changes going on in your body right now, and that will continue over the next few yea—"

"LA LA LA!" I jokingly plug my ears and drown out her words because this is super uncomfortable. Like talking to Vittoria about her period. It's like I *want* to know all about it, but I simultaneously *don't* want to know. Some things it's better not to know too much about until you *have* to know. I imagine many grown-up things are like that, like having a job or pushing a baby out of your *girl parts*.

Anyway, it's like I can sense Mrs. Caldwell trying to dig with a massive drill deep into my soul like only a trained counseling ninja could. This seems like a safe space to open up. What she doesn't know is that today I'm trying to get *her* to open up too.

Nothing seems to make Mrs. Caldwell uncomfortable, ever: not sitting in silence and waiting for me, not my questions, and definitely not staring into my eyes for what feels like hours. She also seems comfortable with—almost unaware of—the very light scar that runs across her left cheek from ear to mouth.

31

I can't keep eye contact any longer, so I look away. She waits patiently. Then, finally: "What would happen if you talked to your mom about some of these questions you have?"

I snort, not on purpose (obviously), but it just comes out.

"Can you talk to your mom?" she presses.

"Sometimes," I say. "Sometimes not."

"Okay," she says. "So is there something specific I can answer for you?"

I have so many specifics. I don't want to be overwhelming. *Stay the course, Serah*, I tell myself. Some of these questions are just *so cringey*.

"What do you want to know?" she patiently asks.

So many things, Mrs. Caldwell. *Too many to count. Why does it seem like it's a lie that beauty is on the inside? And why do my legs seem too skinny to me but perfect to Courtney? Why is thinness so valued? And perfect noses? And breast size?*

"Well, I know I have skinny legs." Let's start with what's easiest. "They're just . . . skinny. It was always okay before. But for some reason, now it seems like it's not. Why are other girls starting to point them out, call me names, and now something that's always been a part of me and normal seems suddenly 'not normal'?"

"Ah, yes," Mrs. Caldwell indicates a light bulb is going off in her mind. "Serah, as girls begin to go through puberty—and they begin before boys—they start to notice the changes in their bodies. Sometimes, girls can grow as many as six inches in one year! Girls your age are beginning to grow breasts, all at varying speeds."

I lean back and cross my arms, trying not to let my face reflect the cringing I'm doing inside—and failing miserably, I'm sure. Mrs. Caldwell pretends she doesn't notice.

"These fast changes can seem sudden and unnerving or overwhelming. Many girls also start to have crushes, and that complicates things, especially because boys aren't typically ready to like girls when girls are ready to like them."

Now I'm cringing with my face.

"Navigating through those feelings can be difficult. All of these things together can cause girls to become self-conscious or act differently, trying to find where they fit in or where they don't. Often, they compare themselves to other girls who are at different points on their journeys through puberty and also might have something they don't—whether it be physical maturity, skills, or gifts. Comparison can end up being really hurtful and can cause insecurity to grow."

Pause. *Is she done?* I wonder to myself.

"What do you think about your legs?" she counters.

"What do you mean?" I haven't really thought about it.

"Well, do they work? Can you walk? Run? Do all the things that God gave you legs to be able to do?"

"Uh, I believe so. Last time I checked, anyway."

"What do you think about that? Their purpose and function?"

"Hmm . . . well, I guess when you put it that way, the fact that they are long makes me a fast and strong runner for soccer."

"Excellent! Anything else?"

"It can be hard to find pants that fit," I say with a wrinkled nose.

She giggles warmly. "I don't know a single person who doesn't struggle to find clothes that fit well! Every brand cuts clothing differently; every store has its own formula. The very fact that they now make slim, regular, plus, tall, and short in a lot of clothing is evidence that retailers are figuring out that one size does not fit all."

"I guess that's true," I respond. "My sister, Vittoria, who doesn't want to take me shopping with her, always seems to complain about most of the clothes she buys, even though she picks them out in the first place. It makes no sense! 'These pants look bad right through here,' or 'My thighs are SO big! These shorts make them look HUGE!'" I mimic in my best Vittoria imitation.

"What do you think of your sister when she says these things?"

"I honestly am not sure what she's complaining about. She looks fine to me. I think she puts a lot of pressure on herself because of dancing."

"And so back to your legs," Mrs. Caldwell refocuses. "Finding pants that fit can be hard, and having long, thin legs helps you run fast. Anything else?"

Christine Virgin

"People call me 'Twiggyphina,'" I say as I look down. At some level, it feels a little strange to complain about my legs when I can see that scar every time I look at her face.

"How does that make you feel?" she asks gently.

"Honestly, it doesn't really bother me much," I say sincerely. "I guess I do like my legs. It's just that I had never really thought about it much before, and now, they seem to be a topic of conversation for some of the girls as if they're discussing something as insignificant as a TikTok dance, but I'm a person."

Mrs. Caldwell thinks for a few seconds before speaking. "Sometimes, it helps me to remember, even as an adult, that when other people put me down for no apparent reason, it's possible they are trying to escape thinking about their own insecurities. Have you ever heard that 'hurting people, hurt people'? In other words, people who are themselves hurting often lash out to cope with their own pain. Or it might be insecurity or stress."

She meets my eyes, and I meet hers back.

"Seraphina, we all have insecurities. It's what we do about them that matters. What's important is to face them and remind yourself of the truth when you start to feel insecure about your legs or anything else: The truth is that God made you, Seraphina Reynolds, different from every single other person who has ever lived. And you, just like every other person on earth, are made in the image of God. It might help to remember, too, that every single woman you know has survived puberty."

I try to let all of that sink in.

"That is slightly comforting. But when does it end? And how do you know it has? When puberty is over, and I'm an adult, is everything going to be easier?"

Mrs. Caldwell laughs. "Wouldn't that be nice? I wish I could promise you that, but I can't," she offers. "It's all a journey. Who you believe yourself to be on the way will matter a lot. There will be plenty of people who will try to make you believe things about yourself that are untrue. It's your choice whether you give them that power."

She truly is a ninja counselor.

I'm not sure if we're done here, and I think about getting up and ending the conversation, but I want to get to Rachel, Plain and Large.

"Mrs. Caldwell?" I ask. I'm determined not to look away.

"Yes, Serah," she says.

"I, well, I talked to this girl at the airport while on spring break. And, well, she was . . . different. She didn't look at all like someone people would notice for her looks in a *good* way, but her dad called her 'beautiful' over and over, and she believed it—like, really believed it, even though she didn't look it."

Pause. "And?"

"And I found it both annoying and sad."

"What about this girl made you annoyed and sad?"

"I guess that she felt beautiful, and I don't," I say as I stare out the window. "But when I compared my looks to hers, I thought, *I'm definitely more pretty than she is.*"

Darn it, Mrs. Caldwell, don't judge me for judging her!

"If she's not beautiful, what is she?" Mrs. Caldwell asks.

"Normal. Plain. Is that bad to say out loud?"
She doesn't answer.

"If you're not beautiful, what are you?" she asks gently, with curiosity.

I don't say any of this out loud; I'm a six or a seven out of ten. I can just tell. If I were on stage for all to judge me, and I had a "hot or not" sash on me, I would probably be voted "not." I have to say something.

"Maybe cute? Not ugly, but not gorgeous like my mom or sister."

"What makes you cute?"

"Well, I think my whole self, like all of me, wrapped into one. My hair, my smile, my heterochromia, my brains, my bounce . . ."

"Is cute good enough?"

"Well, I always liked being called cute. But it isn't the same as pretty or beautiful. Somehow, it seems to matter to me more now than before."

"Can you pinpoint any reason you would feel that cute is 'not enough'?" Mrs. Caldwell asks as she leans toward me and lays a gentle hand on my forearm.

"I'm not sure," I say. And that's the truth.

Mrs. Caldwell meets my eyes, and I decide to meet hers one last time. There's so much more I want to know. That scar . . .

"You are more than enough, Seraphina, a true beauty," Mrs. Caldwell offers in a voice that shows she means it. She's not just saying it. She's doing that thing where she stares deep into my eyes without even blinking.

"Maybe," I say with a shrug. "You might believe that, but . . ." I trail off.

Mrs. Caldwell smiles warmly. "Maybe you don't see it—YET. You may come back anytime, dear Serah, and I hope you will. I'm here for you."

I chicken out, deciding I can come back soon to talk about *her*.

As I say goodbye, I realize I'm feeling better already. And I decide to add puberty to my NOT-Beautiful List.

Chapter 5:
BOY TALK, GIRL TALK

"Into You"
—ARIANA GRANDE

*The best and most beautiful things
in the world cannot be seen or even touched;
they must be felt with the heart.*
—HELEN KELLER

It's Monday, and I don't feel like doing my homework, so I grab my iPod. My parents got me an iPod last year, which has all sorts of limits and restrictions on it. But it means I can use my email address to send text messages. Thank goodness! It feels like most days, I'm the only kid in my entire grade who doesn't have an actual cell phone. I know there are others who don't—because I actually asked everyone individually, and there are eight of us who don't—but it can be absolutely miserable to feel like the only one left. Most of those with a phone also have social media, which my parents just let Vittoria get. From what I've seen so far, it seems like a complete time suck in a bad way. Feeling like I'm missing out on some inside joke among lots of other kids can be isolating. But there's not much I can do about it. My parents pay for the phones and iPods, so I guess the joke's on me. And if it weren't bad enough that I don't have an actual phone, my parents are allowed to maintain and control my address book and read any of my texts. I know my mom has only looked a few times, and I've never had it taken away ('cause I'm such a good kid). 😜

I send Courtney a text.

u there?

Yep

thx for listening this weekend

u bet

And I love ur legs ❯

ha! Love urs more ❯

I'm glad someone does. What's ur favorite thing about ur looks?

Hmm . . . not my legs 😊
maybe my smile? I dunno.
What do you think?

Ur nose hair 🐷
JK. Ur smile is killer

Funny. Ur best feature
is ur leg hair 😊

Shut up! ur lucky that
you can't see urs so much

Oh please! I started shaving
bc according to my mom,
my legs looked like a musk ox.
I didn't show you?
I cut myself all over

NOOOOO! I didn't notice.
Sorry to hear that. Sounds painful

I'm going to try to love my
legs, too, like I love my
heterochromia. that's my
favorite thing about my looks

u should. I'll try too. To love my
legs, not your heteromafia

41

Ha! I wonder if Rachel from
the airport loves her legs

who knows? she prolly doesn't
even think about them. I wonder
if Veruca loves her legs

prolly not. She's so mean, I don't
think she likes herself

did u do math hw yet?
Need any help?

Nope and nope

K, ttyl!

c u tomorrow

◦ ✻ ◦

On Wednesday, I'm stuck after school waiting for
my brother to pick me up once his baseball game ends.
I've finished all my homework and am reading the new
National Geographic when he pulls up.

"Hey, Serah, hop in!" he yells.

"Coming!" I jog to the car, open the back door, and
toss in my heavy backpack, then climb into the front passenger seat.

"How was your game, Alessandro?"

"Personally, not great. I got an error, AND I struck out twice. But I did get an RBI double. And we won, four to three."

"That doesn't sound so bad. Your RBI might have made the difference in the whole game."

"It kinda did. It was the winning run." He smiles sideways at me.

"Alessandro, can I ask you something?"

"Sure, but make it quick. I'm going to drop you off and then head to Ryan's to work on trig together."

"I can probably figure out your trig," I offer as a joke.

"Probably could," he retorts, laughing.

"So, like, do guys, when they're together, generally talk about girls and how hot they are?"

"What? What are you talking about? Why would you think that?"

"Well, last weekend, you, Ryan, and Justin were comparing Beccas and other girls and basically voting on whether they were 'hot or not.'" I use air quotes for emphasis.

"Oh, that. You heard that?"

"I was sitting right there," I say sarcastically. "Vittoria probably heard it, too, seeing as she was in the water with all of you."

"Uh, well . . . I guess we talk about girls that way, not like a lot, but sometimes. Besides, girls do the same thing, don't they?"

"What?! *No!*"

"Oh, please. I've heard Vittoria and her girlfriends gushing about how hot this guy or that guy is and how they want this one or that one to ask her out. They also drool as they scroll through Instagram pics of what they would call hot guys."

"Yeah, okay, I guess you have a point. I guess I'm just wondering about how a girl or a guy's 'hotness' matters."

"I don't know how to explain it, Serah. I think maybe you're too young to understand."

"Nah uh," I say. "That's not fair. I might be twelve, but I understand a LOT, and you should give me more credit than that. Besides, if you're going to talk about girls like that right in front of me, you should be able to explain it," I point out, crossing my arms.

He sighs. "I've never really thought about it. I don't remember starting a conversation about it, but I remember just saying I thought both Beccas were good-looking—"

"Hot, you mean," I interject.

"Okay, fine, HOT, and I'd be happy to date either of them. My buddies asked, and I answered honestly. It just happens. It's guy talk. Everyone does it sometimes."

"Vittoria tells me, 'It's just girl talk,' about a lot of stuff too. I think some of it is just plain dumb."

"I never said it wasn't dumb, but it just happens. Besides, it's not *all* we talk about. It was, like, a one-minute conversation. The way I remember it, Ryan was trying to figure out if he should ask Becca Bromwell to prom. I don't remember it being that bad."

"So it seems like no big deal to consider whether you should date someone based on what she looks like?"

"Well, no . . ." he backtracks. "Ryan and Becca have known each other since sixth grade and have been friends. She's cool." We turn onto our street. "Listen, this has been real, but we're pulling up, and I need to drop you off. I'd rather keep this between you and me. I love you, lil sis, but if you mention this conversation to anyone, I'll deny that it ever happened and then never give you a ride again, okay?"

"Sure, yeah," I say. As I get out and open the back door to grab my backpack, I realize my window of opportunity to ask anything about this topic again is quickly closing. My mind frantic, I stop the car door mid-swing and blurt out, "Alessandro, is hot the same thing as beautiful?"

"Ugh, no, it's not," he says. "Close the door!"

I'm left feeling slightly annoyed, thinking that wasn't much help at all. I think I already knew hot and beautiful were different.

◦ ❀ ◦

Thursdays are my favorite days of the school week. They're one day away from the weekend, and I also have soccer practice.

Soccer makes me feel amazing. My teammates and I work hard and play hard. Learning to work together toward the same goal, carrying each other through mistakes, and celebrating our strengths is empowering. Because I'm a really fast runner, I'm a midfielder. Soccer is something in my life that makes "fiery-winged" make sense to me. Literally, I can have bursts of speed that make it seem like an engine is running inside me, firing pistons to make me go. I can get the ball to my teammates so they can score. I love making a great assist. But I'd be lying if I said assists feel as good as goals. This season, I've scored two goals over six games, which is okay. Courtney has *five*. She's a forward. I envy her a little because of it. She knows. I should remember to point out to her that her awesome legs are partially responsible for her five goals.

We don't get to see each other during the school day much because our schedules are different. So soccer practice is a time to catch up—which, today, makes me a little nervous.

I don't want Courtney to mention ANYTHING about what we've shared with each other recently, and I don't want her to ask about Rachel in front of the other girls. I would be so embarrassed! As I wonder if any of the other girls on the team are insecure about anything, I casually approach Courtney like it's any old day. I'm grateful that Liv and Katie are busy talking about boys. I listen long enough to hear one of them go on and on about how "dreamy" someone is, which makes me cringe thinking about the conversation I *just* had with Alessandro. Liv's actual name is Olivia, which means "symbol of peace." Katie's name is Katherine, which means "pure." Both of their names are sometimes true and sometimes not—which, come to think of it, could be true for all names and people. Diana is out sick today.

"Hey, Court!" I say, almost a little too loudly. "How are things since I last texted an hour ago?"

"The same, my friend," she says. "You ready to run?" Court says this to me at the start of every practice, and today, I understand the signal she is sending; she's not going to embarrass me in front of everyone. It's just a normal Thursday. I am so relieved.

As practice begins, I chase the ball and do my drills, but my mind wanders, thinking about what the other girls might be self-conscious about. Most of them seem so confident. Are they all insecure on the inside, at least about *something*? I probably seem confident to them too. And I usually am. I doubt anyone out here other than Courtney has any idea that my breasts or my legs are on my mind. Could it be possible that many of these girls are wondering about the same things? Or different things in the same way? It's unusually hot for an April afternoon, so Coach Snyder sends us for a water break early.

"Liv, so, like, I saw you talking to Corey today," Katie says, batting her eyelashes at Olivia.

"Oh, do tell!" Courtney chimes in.

"It was nothing!" Liv says, blushing.

"It didn't look like nothing," Katie giggles. "Your face got red like it's getting red right now."

"Okay, okay. He elbowed my head as he sat down at his desk in social studies and then said, 'I'm sorry, Liv, are you okay?' as he rubbed my head where he hit me."

"Oooooh!" Katie squeals with delight.

"I knew you'd do this," Liv says. "You're so boy crazy!"

"No, I'm not; I just think it's cute that you have a crush on Corey, and he has a crush on you."

"He is super cute, but he *doesn't* have a crush on me," Liv emphatically denies as she buries her face in her hands.

"Yes, he does! I asked him if he liked anybody, and he said no, but then when I pushed and started asking one by one with names, he said no to each name I mentioned until I got to your name, and he looked at me like, 'Oh come on, why are you doing this to me?' and didn't answer. *Then* I asked Nick if Corey liked you, and he said yes."

"Wow, and here I am, thinking Serah's the queen of investigations," Courtney inserts. "The real question is who *Nick* likes. Did you get around to asking that while you were busy interrogating him about Corey?"

"Nope, that's your job. I'm done," Katie holds up her hands to show she gives in. "Besides, I don't have any crushes right now."

"Who are you, and what have you done with our friend Katie?" I demand.

"Oh, please," she says as Coach calls us back to the field. As I run back out, I shake my head, thinking about Katie and how she is always talking about crushes. She didn't use to be like this, and I realize this is changing too. I'm glad I'm not boy crazy. It probably helps that Alessandro and his friends smell bad; they and the boys in my class seem completely uninteresting to me—except maybe Seth Rodriguez. But only Courtney knows this, and she is sworn to secrecy.

Chapter 6:

ZITS AND PUBIC HAIR

"Live Like You're Loved"
—HAWK NELSON

Beauty is not in the face; beauty is a light in the heart.
—KAHLIL GIBRAN

The next Friday after school, I'm not at a friend's house. I'm in the waiting room at the dermatologist's office with my mom, who's skimming a fashion magazine. I haven't had a chance to finish the latest *National Geographic*, so I'm about halfway through it when my mind wanders to where I'd rather be—at Courtney's or Liv's or Katie's or Jessica's, who is my favorite school friend.

Jessica is in most of my classes, and if she were into *National Geographic*, she could read it and understand all of it just like I do. Even though people don't talk about it that much, we all know we are broken up into our classes based on how well we perform in the various subject areas.

Jessica and I have been in the same core subject classes since third grade.

Teachers don't tell us they've split us up this way, but we just know it. When you go to school with the same kids since kindergarten, you learn who can answer all the math questions right away and who can't. There are some kids who raise their hands with confidence and have the answers, and then there are the kids who get called on and wish they hadn't. The teachers don't talk about it, but it's pretty obvious you can't read as well as someone else when your book in third grade is skinny with lots of pictures and big print, and your friend's is a 150-page chapter book. And it makes sense that people learn in different ways at different speeds. I think this is another example of how we're all unique. It's just like anything, really. Some kids pick up a sport instantly, while others don't even want to try because it feels so hard. And the worst standardized test of all time has to be the mile run. We all have to do it, but the same kids come in first, year after year. And the same kids come in last. It's impossible not to compare.

No matter how much our teachers tell us to have a growth mindset, it's weird to hear my friends say things to me like, "I'm in the low math class." Sometimes, when a teacher calls on someone, she'll say, "I don't know, ask Serah; she knows *everything*." I enjoy hanging out with Jessica because she doesn't make me feel bad for being the student I am. Liv is constantly complaining about how her parents are going to ground her or even give away her dog if she doesn't get better grades. They want her to work harder so she can move into a more advanced math class to help with college. I mean, we're in SIXTH GRADE! We're barely starting puberty, and her parents are worried about something that won't happen until she is legally an adult. With some friends, like Courtney—who is in my math class but generally not in my others (which *kills* us both)—I know it doesn't bother her that reading is a little more challenging for her. It goes both ways. I can be happy for her that she's scored five goals but also a little envious, and that's okay.

This makes me wonder if it's the same with all sorts of gifts. Maybe Serena and Venus Williams have felt guilty at some point about their success. That seems like a ridiculous thought because I'm sure they've both worked very, very hard. But there are probably other tennis players who have worked as hard but aren't as good. I wonder how many people have *tried* to make the Williams sisters feel bad for their talent. Maybe beautiful people feel guilty about being beautiful. When we "cute girls" gush and say, "Wow, she's so beautiful; I'll never look like that," does that make the beautiful person feel bad?

I am interrupted by getting called to the room for my appointment. The nurse measures my height and weighs me, takes my blood pressure and temperature. As she's doing these things, she tells me she is going to be the one examining my whole body to look at all of my moles before the dermatologist does. Thank goodness it's her and not the male doctor. My mom insisted we see this particular guy because he's the best. 🌚

51

I strip down to my underwear, which suddenly seems embarrassing, not only because it says "Tuesday" and it's a Friday, but also because it has a picture of a unicorn on it. The boys at school have outgrown Legos and Minecraft and have moved on to Fortnight. We girls have outgrown princesses, My Little Pony, and (clearly) Hello Kitty. But am I too old for unicorns now? I love unicorns! I also wasn't expecting that a stranger would be looking at them on my underpants when I put them on this morning.

I realize that, of course, the nurse hasn't noticed them at all. She examines almost all of my body, lifting my arms and checking my armpits, running her fingers through my hair to see my scalp and even in between my toes. She has my mom check my *very* private areas for moles. I turn my backside to my mom so that she can pull down my underpants in the back, away from the nurse's view. As I pull on the elastic at the front of my underpants to look for moles "down there," my mom takes a quick peek as well. My realization comes at the exact moment as her shriek.

"Seraphina, you've grown pubic hair! LOTS of it!!!"

In one second, I feel my face turn fire engine red as I mumble something to the nurse about waiting outside for a minute. She understands what I'm trying to say, even if the words were jumbled together, because she says, "Of course," and leaves, closing the door behind her. As soon as she's gone, I swing my head toward my mom as fast as my neck will move it, and with my mouth open in despair, all I can manage is, "What the heck?!"

"Sorry, I just didn't know!" my mom fires back. She sounds—strangely—both delighted and shocked, based on the decibel level of her voice. "Why didn't you tell me that had started?" pointing toward my crotch as if it's guilty of committing a crime.

"Um, I didn't know this was information I needed to share with you?" I squeal 'cause I'm trying to indicate I'm yelling at her without yelling, so no one else will hear. "Maybe if you had made it clear before those hairs ever started growing that you needed to know, I might have said something! Why do you have to embarrass me so much?!"

"I said I'm sorry!" she says almost meaningfully. I can tell she's trying so hard not to smile, but it breaks through, along with some blush on her cheeks.

How dare she think my embarrassment is funny!

"It just means . . . well . . . my baby's growing up is all." Her shoulders relax, and her voice softens. "I guess you just caught me off-guard. I am sorry I embarrassed you."

"*I* caught *you* off-guard? I'm not the one looking in your underpants! Can we please forget about this and move on, Mom? Did you see any moles?" I've lowered my voice substantially, crawling off the ledge of mortification.

"No, sweetie, I didn't. I think you're fine."

At this moment, the nurse knocks, making it obvious that she's been listening at the door the whole time and now knows it's safe to return and get back to business. When she opens the door, she pokes her head in just far enough to confirm I don't have any moles near my hoo-haw, to let me know I can put my clothes back on, and to say the doctor will be in to see us in a minute. Her head is gone just as quickly as it entered, like a turtle sticking its neck out just long enough to see the danger outside before retreating back into its shell.

◦ ❁ ◦

"Your moles all look great, Seraphina," Dr. Kendall says. My mom looks relieved to hear this.

"And what about the pimples here and there?" my mom asks.

"Well, tell me about your skincare routine," Dr. Kendall asks, looking at me.

"That's easy. I don't have one."

"Ah. Well, for many girls your age, it's a good time to start thinking about how to take care of that beautiful face of yours."

"Do you say that to all your patients, Dr. Kendall?"

"Not all of them."

"All of your twelve-year-old patients?" I raise my eyebrow.

He grins. "Just the ones who have acne." I cringe, realize he's got me, and he laughs. "I'm joking! Just the beautiful ones." He's good. He's also handsome and not very old, which means I blush a little but am determined not to miss a beat and embarrass myself. I've had enough for one day between my unicorn underpants and pubic hair reveal.

"Tell me what to do," I say in my most let's-get-on-with-it voice.

"Well, as I was saying . . . at your age, it's a good idea to begin cleansing and moisturizing twice a day."

My mind wanders as it dawns on me that every *single* doctor's appointment is changing now that I'm twelve. "Can you ride a bike?" "Are you switching feet when you climb stairs?" "Can you read these letters on the wall?" It used to be so much simpler.

"Your pores are more prone to getting clogged now and are excreting more oils."

Fantastic.

"I have some samples of various over-the-counter cleansers and moisturizers I like to give my new preteen patients so they can try them all for a week or two and then pick the one that works best for them. If you start to get dry or irritated skin from any one of these, stop using it and try a different one."

Is he saying my skin might actually get worse rather than better?

"You don't have a lot of acne, so starting a skincare regimen now will serve you well and help minimize your acne over the next several years." I'm listening. "If your face erupts in an amount of acne that makes you self-conscious"—I'm now picturing my face as a surface full of tiny, active volcanoes—"or if you begin to have painful acne, just have your mom schedule another appointment, and you can come back so we can look at other treatment options." He pauses and looks at my mom, then back at me again.

"For now, just keep flashing that pretty smile and find your favorite cleanser and moisturizer and use them both every morning and night. Sound good?"

He seems to be moving at warp speed. I'm trying to process all he's saying. I might have painful acne? Or acne that makes me self-conscious? Aren't I already self-conscious enough? And how long am I supposed to use a face wash before switching and trying another one?

"Uh-huh, sure," I say. I decide I'll ask Vittoria to show me what she does *exactly*, so I can make sure I'm doing it right. That or there's got to be a YouTube video for it. This guy is really nice and cute and flattering, so it would be too embarrassing to ask him how to wash my face and how much moisturizer to rub in.

"Do you have any more questions for me, Seraphina or Elenore?"

My mom has been surprisingly—and to my relief—quiet. Now that she's been called on, she has a question.

"Will regular over-the-counter cleansers clear up the acne that Serah does have? Is there one you recommend that she try out first because it will be most effective with her skin type?"

"Some acne is generally a part of puberty for almost all kids, no matter how great of a routine they have or which cleansers they use. There is no true cure for acne, as you know. It is definitely more about management. If Serah's skin hasn't historically been too sensitive, she should try one of the cleansers containing salicylic acid or benzoyl peroxide. Generally, one or the other tends to work better for most. But a completely clear face, especially as Seraphina begins menstruating, is probably unrealistic."

For heaven's sake, please get me out of here. I can feel my face getting red and hot. Please don't let them start discussing when I should get girl flu. Please, please, please. That is not something a dermatologist deals with, is it? Why is my gorgeous skin doctor talking about Aunt Flo? I pretend there is something in my purse I desperately need so that no one will look at me. With the way today is going, the panty liner I carry in there will probably fall out on the table as an exclamation point to the extraordinarily embarrassing past hour.

"I figured that's what you would say," my mom continues. "I just wanted to be sure. I remember trying all sorts of things to keep my own pimples in check throughout my teen years. Vittoria seems to be doing well, just the odd pimple here and there. I hope Seraphina will be blessed in the same way."

"That would be a blessing indeed, but who knows? Seraphina, just remember you're not bad at taking care of yourself or 'dirty' for having acne. I had terrible acne as a teenager, and I still have scars if you look closely at my skin. It's why I became a dermatologist."

If I could bring myself to look at him since he said the word "menstruating," I would get close enough to see his scars. I seriously just want to get out of here without him noticing my red cheeks.

"Mom, are you ready to go?" I turn my face just enough to make eye contact, silently pleading with her through my expression.

"Yes, Serah, let's head out. Thank you, Dr. Kendall."

"You betcha."

Chapter 7:
FAMILY DINNER

"Daughters"

—JOHN MAYER

Beauty is how you feel inside, and it reflects in your eyes. It is not something physical.

—SOPHIA LOREN

Back at home, I trudge up the stairs and dump out the contents of my samples bag onto the bathroom counter. I take a quick peek in the mirror and notice my face looks like it's finally back to its usual color. I lean in really close to see my zits. There are only about a dozen. But they seem like a very savage part of puberty. I'm adding them to the list of "definitely not beautiful" things.

I look over at Vittoria's sink, where pretty bottles of toner (whatever that is), cleanser, moisturizer, and night cream are neatly lined up next to the sink. There's also a row of fancy perfumes that either my mom handed down to her or maybe she took, knowing the woman would never notice. I open the first bottle and hold it up to my nose. It smells super floral, sort of like an old lady, and I quickly put the cap back on. The next one is sort of earthy and woodsy and fresh. The third smells very citrusy and sweet, like vanilla. I decide to add a squirt of it to my wrist, and at that very moment, Vittoria walks in.

"What are you doing, you little brat? Who said you could use those?"

"Oh please, Vittoria! Does Mom even know you have these?"

Vittoria's face twists out of its stern "I caught you red-handed" look into one of surprise.

"Yes, as a matter of fact, she does."

"Oh really? Mooooom!" I call as loudly as I can out the bathroom door.

"Shut up, Serah, you've made your point. Fine. I don't care if you try the perfume; just ask first, okay?" As I think about how hypocritical that seems, I choose not to say anything else about "her" perfumes so I can get what I need.

"Vittoria, I'm actually glad you're here. Dr. Kendall gave me these face washes and moisturizers to try. I don't know which one to try first or really how to wash my face."

"So now you want my help?" she sneers. Then she backs off a bit. I think she sees this as a proud big sister moment, like getting to impart expertise about one of three things she cares deeply about—fashion, looks, and boys. And not necessarily in that order.

"Mom took you to see Dr. Hot, huh?"

I nod, yet again remembering my conversation with Alessandro, not wanting to agree out loud but also not capable of saying no. I mean, he was very good-looking.

"Well, I'm not really ready to wash my face for the night right *now*, but I can show you later tonight if you want. When Cecilia comes to sleep over, we're going to put masks on. If you don't do anything that bothers us before that, you can join us."

"Can I put on a mask too?"

"You're serious?"

"Why not?"

"Because we're going to be talking about fifteen-year-old stuff, and you're eleven."

"You're fourteen, not fifteen, and I'm TWELVE."

"See? That's exactly why you can't hang out with us. You're so annoying!"

"Fine, I'll leave you alone. I don't care about hearing all about how you both want to make out with Josh Swanson and then listen to you practice acting it out on your pillows anyway."

She ignores my comment completely—adding truth to what was until this moment only a guess on my part about their plans—and she changes the subject back to Dr. Hot.

"Mom took me to Dr. Kendall in sixth grade too. I didn't even have any pimples yet, but she wanted me to go for 'preventative care.'"

"Your skin looks really good, so maybe it worked."

It's always a good idea to butter up your older sister when you need something from her.

"Yeah, maybe." She seems lost in thought. I imagine she is daydreaming about Josh because I brought him up. Then, we hear the call to dinner.

◎ ❊ ◎

It is usually spontaneous when our whole family is together for dinner. My dad's so often at the hospital or the office at dinnertime, and with our activities, there's a lot of coming and going. Tonight is a rare moment we are all sitting down and eating together. My mom's never really been a cook, except for on holidays. She will spend three straight days preparing enough food for an army when she will be hosting ten to fifteen people. Her mantra has always been, "I make a mean reservation." 🙂 Our takeout choice tonight is Chinese.

Alessandro and I dig in while Vittoria sits and studies the spread. She adds one teeny scoop of rice to her plate and then counts out ten steamed broccoli trees and six pieces of steamed chicken. She begins eating them dry, without sauce.

I look at my mom, who seems to have noticed as well.

"Vittoria, tell us about your day," Mom says.

"It was fine."

"Did anything interesting happen?"

"Not really. I'm interested in finishing dinner so Cecilia and I can go to the movies." My mom gives her a look that indicates this is not the interesting fact about her day that she was hoping to hear. Vittoria tries again. "Joey Wright got sent to the principal today for comparing Mrs. Wood's name to something inappropriate in class."

Alessandro gives a weak laugh, then coughs as he realizes he's not supposed to. I can tell I've missed something completely.

"How are your grades, Vittoria?" Dad asks, both to change the subject and because he always asks about our grades.

"Good."

"How good?" he persists.

"Good enough, Dad," Vittoria retorts, but it's not good enough at all.

"Tell me what they are. In what classes do you have As right now?"

"All of them but Spanish and math."

"What are your Spanish and math grades?" He is relentless.

"I think a B and a B minus."

"Well, a B is okay, but the B minus . . . do you need extra help? Or perhaps we should cut back on some of those dance classes you're taking so you can focus more on your studies."

I'm reminded of Liv, and I genuinely feel bad for Vittoria. This is like the Salem Witch Hunt. Well, maybe not quite, but close enough.

"I'm fine, Dad," Vittoria says, looking down at her remaining bland food. "Genevieve said she'll help me."

"Okay, but if you don't get those grades up, I'll stop paying for dance."

"What about you, Alessandro?" My mom glares at my dad and attempts to change the subject. "Tell us about your day."

"It was uneventful. I had school. They handed out the forms for the last SAT tests this spring. I know you guys want me to take it one more time, so I'll pick a Saturday when baseball doesn't conflict and sign up."

"It will be good to have one more shot at raising your score," my dad chimes in. "Mrs. Carnes said if you could get even thirty or forty points higher, it would make a difference for your college applications."

"That's the third time you've told me that, Dad," Alessandro says. "I know."

"And, Seraphina, how about you?"

"I went to the dermatologist because my zits are bothering Mom," I offer.

Dad and Mom look at each other.

"They don't bother me," my mom says, acting offended. The Italian in her kicks in, and her arms start flailing. "You don't have to go to the dermatologist. I thought you might want to start a skincare regimen. I'm sorry if that bothers you and that my care and concern are annoying."

"Mom took us when we were in fifth grade, too, Serah-boo," Alessandro chimes in. "It's a rite of passage."

"What is it with you all?! I'm in SIXTH grade, Alessandro, and I am twelve years old," I slowly and loudly affirm. I huff. "It was embarrassing. Dr. Kendall used the word 'menstruating,' and I wanted to crawl into a hole."

This gets some giggles, but Vittoria understands my pain.

"That's pretty mortifying, especially because Dr. Kendall is hot."

"I know, right?" I say in protest. Immediately Alessandro turns his head toward me, raising one eyebrow in a judgmental stare as if to say, *I caught you using the word hot!* I decide not to say anything else and turn my gaze back to my mom to avoid facing him. Thankfully, my mom saves me from the heavy silence—until I hear the words coming out of her mouth, getting louder with every word.

"You know, I spend so much time trying to help you kids out and do the right thing. And it just backfires. I was doing something *nice* for you today. But it's fine. I will *never* take you to the dermatologist again!" She is now yelling. "Does that make you happy, Serah?!"

"Whoa, whoa, whoa, let's everybody calm down," my dad offers. "Serah, I'm sorry you were embarrassed, but your mom was only trying to help you. When it's time to go back to the dermatologist again, we can schedule your appointment with a female doctor. Sound good?"

"But Dr. Kendall is the BEST!" my mom implores.

"Honey, sometimes, the best is not the best. Let's choose our battles wisely," he manages to say very gently, which calms her down somewhat, but I can tell she is angry and thinking my dad should listen to his own advice.

Just because his battle about grades and SATs wasn't loud doesn't mean it wasn't the same thing.

"Yes, Dad. Thanks," I say.

"Wow, I really wish Cecilia would get here," Vittoria mutters under her breath but clearly enough that all of us can understand her. We eat in silence for a few minutes, probably because no one wants to cause any more conflict. I finish quickly, grab one of the six fortune cookies from the pile, and crack it open. I have *got* to find a way to lighten things up. I feel a little guilty, like the silence is my fault.

"Your siblings secretly worship you," I say out loud, pretending to read it from my little fortune. My mom questions gullibly, "Is that really what it says?" as Alessandro grabs at it from across the table, knowing that can't be what it says. I'm not fast enough nor far enough away to keep him from getting his quick hands on it, and we both giggle as he grabs it.

"Ahem," he reads with a big to-do, "A closed mouth gathers no feet. That's actually a good one for you, Serah-boo."

"Very funny," I say. "Let's see what you get."

He picks a cookie from the pile, pops the bag in one hand while simultaneously crushing his cookie into little bits, and fishes out the tiny paper.

"'That wasn't chicken,'" he reads and then gets a grossed-out expression on his face. To me, this is hilarious.

"Okay, is that also a joke or really what it says?" My mom can't help it.

"See for yourself." Alessandro hands it over to her. Sure enough, it really does say that. Now my mom, dad, and Vittoria are curious, each grabbing one of the remaining cookies.

"You will live long enough to open many fortune cookies," my dad reads with a grin.

"Someone is looking up to you. Don't let that person down," my mom reads, sounding lost in thought.

"In youth and beauty, wisdom is rare," Vittoria adds, then shows her distaste for this entire experience by rolling her eyes.

"Anyone not going to eat theirs?" Alessandro asks no one in particular, hoping he can have any undesired cookies.

"You can have mine," Vittoria says.

"There's a surprise," I add, smirking. She gives me a death glare, and I backpedal, not wanting her to go back on letting me spend time with her and Cecilia.

"You've never liked fortune cookies, is all."

"That's true," she says, and her glare softens. She looks down at her cell phone, pushes her chair back, and says, "It's been fun, but Cecilia's mom is here. You're going to get us from the movies at ten, right, Mom?"

"Yep, I'll be there."

The rest of us begin clearing the table and putting the containers with leftovers into the fridge. When it's all cleaned up, my brother heads to a friend's, and my parents put on one of their shows in the living room. I sit down with them and pull the sixth and final fortune cookie out of my pants pocket.

When Alessandro was busy reading my first fortune to everyone, I took the chance to sneak a second cookie after calculating we would have an extra. I carefully open it before savoring every broken piece.

"Ask your mom instead of a cookie," it reads. *These things are worthless*, I think to myself.

Chapter 8:
MEAN GIRLS

"Girlfriend"
—AVRIL LAVIGNE

*Like a gold ring in a pig's snout is a
beautiful woman who shows no discretion.*

—PROVERBS 11:22

I'm falling asleep on the couch when my mom returns with Cecilia and Vittoria. They come in all giggly, bursting with laughter about what happened at the movies. I watch them through my peripheral vision, not wanting to seem too interested in what they're up to. Without moving my head too much, I watch them raid the kitchen for snacks. My sister finds some rice cakes, and Cecilia grabs some chips. They lower their voices as they crack open sparkling waters. My mom reminds them to go to sleep at a reasonable hour, says good night to us all, and turns in.

I have to make my move very carefully. They seem very happy, so it seems like a good time to insert myself into their sleepover. But I don't want to seem too eager or pushy, or they'll lock themselves in Vittoria's room to avoid me like the plague. I have to play my cards just right.

I casually get up and head to the kitchen to test the waters. I open the fridge door, looking for a snack of my own, and I pull out some leftover lo mein. I begin eating right from the carton and stand there quietly: Phase one of my plan is to show them I can be with them and stay cool.

"I still can't believe you did that!" Vittoria says.

"I know . . . I can't either. Did you see her *face*?!" Cecilia gushes.

"Umm, yeah! How could I miss it? It got *soooo* pink and embarrassed."

"And then she looked at Josh for help, and he did NOTHING. I would have been so mad at him! I wonder if it will make her mad enough to break up with him?"

"I don't know . . . they both looked so . . . stunned. Speechless, even," Vittoria replies. "Do you want to take these snacks upstairs with us? We can keep eating in my room, as long as this one over here can keep her mouth shut." Vittoria motions her head toward me, acknowledging my presence for the first time but also feeling out whether I will be on her side tonight.

"Of course!" I say eagerly, "I won't say a word, as long as we can go upstairs and do some masks before you shut yourselves in your room . . ." I immediately question my response, wishing I could take it back. I hold my breath, wondering if I might have overplayed my hand. Maybe I should have just robotically nodded my head and waited for a better moment to propose face washing. My noodles hang down from my fork, hovering above their carton as I wait as still as an antelope in the Serengeti who has just sensed a predator.

"Oh, uh, sure," Vittoria says as she looks at Cecilia. "You don't care if we show Serah how to wash her face, do you?"

"I *guess* not."

"Great! I'll head up to the bathroom and pick out a face wash to try. See you there!" I run off to the stairs before they can change their minds.

The more you tell yourself to just "be cool," the more uncool things come out. I remind myself to relax and not open my mouth unless I'm 100 percent sure that what I'm about to say is indeed legit. I take a few deep breaths to calm my nerves. I don't even know why I feel so much pressure. I wait patiently in the bathroom, trying not to do anything embarrassing like fart and make the bathroom stink. Chinese food gives me gas. Luckily, they arrive a few minutes later with their little mud mask packets, all business. I put the toilet lid down and use it as a stool.

"Serah, give us a sec to take off our makeup, which is *obviously* a step you don't need to worry about for right now," as if to remind me of our age difference and of all the things they get to do that I don't. While they do this, I watch in silence for a few seconds before my curiosity gets the best of me. The words are out of my mouth before I've had the chance to stop them.

"What happened at the movies tonight?"

They stop wiping their eyes with cotton pads, and both look at me. "I'll tell you what happened if you promise me you owe me one the next time I ask you to do anything. Pinky swear?" Vittoria raises an eyebrow at me.

"Pinky swear." We lock pinkies, indicating there's no going back now.

"So we ran into Josh Swanson and Allie White at the movies."

"Does your sister even know who these people are?" Cecilia looks to Vittoria.

"I know who Josh is," I chime in a bit defensively, adding a wink.

"Well, we saw them in line to buy food," Cecilia continues. "I grabbed Vittoria's arm and, like, dragged her over to them as she tried to pull away. She had no idea what I was about to do." They stop to laugh at the memory yet again, then compose themselves. Cecilia continues.

"I walked right up to Josh and Allie and said, 'Josh, hi, are you two shipped up?' He looked at us both and said, 'Yeah, uh, Allie, do you know Cecilia and Vittoria?'" They stop and laugh again at Cecilia's impression of Josh's voice.

"Do you think Allie knows that you have a crush on Josh?" I ask.

"Well, she might know now after what *Cecilia* did!" my sister yells, though I can't tell if she's pretending to be angry or actually is. Knowing my sister, she looks torn. Cecilia picks up the story.

"So I look back at Josh and say, 'Wow, Josh, your girl-friend's really pretty. Pretty ugly.'"

At this, Cecilia bursts out laughing again, and Vittoria joins her, only now Vittoria's laugh sounds strained and forced.

I don't laugh at all. I imagine being Allie in that moment. What did she do? Does Cecilia, or Vittoria for that matter, think Josh is going to be interested in her after doing *that*?

I feel a little sick to my stomach.

Cecilia, sensing my quietness and probably seeing my disdain at what she'd done written all over my face, offers, "They didn't say anything back, of course. We walked away because it got super awkward. But boy, it was funny to see their faces."

I gaze at the sink, truly not knowing what to say, wondering if I'm about to upchuck a bunch of Chinese take-out. If someone said that to me, it wouldn't matter if I were Rachel, Plain and Large. It would have hurt me. If I were confident enough to put my name on my Beautiful List, I might have gone home and erased it. I wonder if Allie is home now, telling her mom—or her sister or brother or best friend—what happened. I imagine her crying.

Vittoria breaks the silence with soft words.

"Serah, do you still want us to show you how to wash your face? We can do that now," she says, almost eagerly.

73

"You know, I'm really tired all of a sudden," I hear myself say. "Vittoria, you can show me another time." Suddenly, a YouTube video about face washing sounds just fine. I feel my legs push me to stand from the toilet as if I'm on autopilot. The movement makes my stomach rumble. I smile devilishly as I realize a takeout food fart is coming out whether I want it to or not. Before I walk through the door, I crop dust them with the stench.

◉ ❀ ◉

The next morning it's raining. I stay in my room with my music and *Nat Geo*, and I relay the whole incident to Courtney through a FaceTime call.

"That's pretty lame of her, I think," Court says. "I'm kind of surprised your sister would do that. Maybe Allie is really mean too?"

"I have no idea. My sister didn't say anything about Allie deserving it or being a jerk. And Court, I could see the embarrassment on Vittoria's face. Cecilia is clearly a warthog. I looked up her name, and it means 'blind.'"

"Not just any piglike wild animal, but a *blind* warthog, huh?"

"I was just reading about desert warthogs in Kenya."

"Of course you were, you nerd."

"Thanks for that."

"Anytime. Let's stop talking about her. Are you ready for our game today?"

"I am; what about you?"

74

"I am. I'm a little nervous. Stoneham is so good!"

"I know, but we're pretty good too. As soon as I start to feel nervous, I remind myself that nothing could be as bad as my visit to the dermatologist yesterday."

"That story is so cringey, Serah. Thanks for the visual of you in unicorn underpants. It's just what I need to get me through the game."

"Bite me. We can beat Stoneham this time. You're not even going to need that image to help, but I'll let you use it if it means you'll score a winning goal."

"Alright, I'll see you there. Peace out."

"C-ya," I say and lose myself in my *Nat Geo* again. It always calms me before a match.

⊙ ❋ ⊙

Not only does my sister tag along to my soccer game but Cecilia comes as well. I'm super thrilled. NOT!

Apparently, Cecilia's mom is going to get her from the field. It doesn't take long before I figure out why they've come. Josh Swanson's sister plays for Stoneham. Clearly, they're hoping to run into him. Or maybe just swoon at him from across the field. If I were them, I would be too embarrassed to ever talk to him again and would try to find a new crush. But I remind myself for what seems like the tenth time in as many days: What do I know?

It has been one of the wettest springs on record, and they almost called the game because the fields are so saturated. But our league plays pretty much rain or shine. I'm sure all the parents love it. The good news is it has stopped raining. But everyone is carrying umbrellas, wearing rain-coats and wellies. Everyone except Cecilia, who's wearing tight, cutoff jean shorts, a VS Pink tank, and is all but ruining her Tory Burch sandals. At least Vittoria is wear-ing somewhat more appropriate attire, having donned rain boots and a hoodie with her cutoffs.

Josh has, in fact, come to watch his sister's game. As I'm finishing warm-ups, I notice Cecilia and Vittoria whis-pering and giggling together and then going back to their phones. A few minutes later, they start walking around the field to the Stoneham side. The game hasn't started yet, so I watch them, wanting to see the train wreck. Josh is sitting in a portable camping chair, doing something on his phone. He's probably doodling devil horns on a pic of Cecilia.

To my surprise, they don't go up to talk to him.

"Yo, Serah, you going to get that practice ball or just stand on the field today?" my coach yells.

"Sorry!" I run after the stray pass I completely missed. I need to get my mind on the game 'cause it's about to start. I take one glance back and realize they've stopped walking. They stand directly in front of Josh's view of the field.

The referees blow their whistles to start the game. I get into place in left midfield, so I'm not far from my sister. I look her way and roll my eyes then immediately look back to the field, not knowing if she saw me.

Stoneham is a great team, and the wet field adds to the physicality of the game. These girls play tough like we do, and we're pretty evenly matched. Ball control is harder on a drenched field. Players are falling and sliding all over the place. Liv misses a pass, and a Stoneham girl takes advantage. She dribbles and shoots unexpectedly from twenty yards out, but we're lucky Katie saw it coming. She's a really good goalie and will probably be our MVP this season.

The game goes like this through the first half—a lot of missed passes, out-of-bounds balls, and close calls. We're all covered in mud from the waist down from kicking and running. The score is tied at zero when we start the second half. I noticed that Cecilia and Vittoria didn't try to talk to Josh at halftime but rather went to the food truck and got snacks.

Stoneham comes back in the game aggressively, and we're put on the defensive. This girl named Alicia Wheeler—who I imagine will probably end up playing for UNC and be on the US women's team someday—is near our goal, and we're defending hard, trying to get the ball away. But she's *so good*. One girl misses her pass from Alicia, and I take advantage when the ball comes right to me. I grab it and break away up the left-field line. I'm looking for a good pass, but nobody is open, so I keep running with a girl named Cindy on my heels. Still, no one is open. As I check the field, I realize I'm getting close to where Vittoria and Cecilia are watching. In a split second, I realize I'm drilling the ball hard out of bounds.

It happens so fast; I can't describe it as anything but instinct. The chip shot whizzes straight at Cecilia, who thankfully happens to be watching the game instead of looking at her phone or drooling at Josh. She has a split second to move out of the way. The ball just misses her and heads farther away from the field down the sideline.

Perhaps to be helpful, but more likely to get Josh's attention, she turns to run after the ball—only, as she pivots, her left sandal slides in the mud. Her legs part like she's a gymnast going down for a split. It seems like slow motion as the crowd can't help but watch Cecilia's fall. The only person not witnessing the train wreck is the generous fan who runs after the ball. Cecilia thrusts her arms in front of her to brace herself, but they slide forward through the muck, and she ends up on her knees and elbows in the muddy grass.

Vittoria rushes to help her up, but the damage is done. Her tank and jean shorts are still clean, but her hands and forearms, lower legs, and sandals are covered in sticky mud. I notice a few snickers and sneers from the sideline, definitely people who are wondering what this girl was thinking dressing like this.

As she pulls herself to standing with Vittoria's help, Vittoria takes one look at her and bursts out laughing. She quickly covers her mouth and looks bashful, not wanting to add insult to injury. Cecilia seems furious but is smart enough to keep her mouth shut as she wipes at the mud all over her. I have only a second to giggle and enjoy it before Stoneham throws the ball back in, and it's game on.

I steal one last look at the sideline as play begins and lock eyes with Josh, who's giving me a thumbs-up. I turn away to get my head back in the game. I'm still not sure whether my foot slipped or if I drilled the ball at Cecilia on purpose. What I do know for sure is that I'm glad my turnover didn't cost the game 'cause we won two to one. And, more importantly, I know where Cecilia's name goes on my Beautiful List.

Chapter 9:
VITTORIA'S STRUGGLE

"Pretty Hurts"

—BEYONCÉ

It's so important to stay anchored in the fact that God made you to be you, and he made you irreplaceable.

—RILEY CLEMMONS, FAN Q&A, CITIZEN OF HEAVEN TOUR, COLUMBUS, OHIO

Later that night, Vittoria knocks on my door.

"Come in."

"Hey, Serah, I can show you how to wash your face now if you want."

"Sure, that'd be fine," I say in a monotone. I follow her into the bathroom quietly.

"I want you to know I apologized to Josh today," Vittoria starts off. I say nothing.

"At your game. Once Cecilia's mom came, I figured I could talk to Josh alone if he was there. I'm glad I had that chance."

"Okay."

"I feel really bad about what happened yesterday, and I just wanted you to know. I had no idea Cecilia was going to do that to Allie."

"Thanks for letting me know," I say quietly. "I do think the person you need to apologize to most of all is Allie."

"That's what Josh said, and I know. I just have to wait until I see her. But I plan on it." She looks at the floor. "Josh said we can still be friends."

"Does Cecilia like Josh as much as you do?"

"I think she likes him *more* than I do." Pause. "It's probably hard for you to understand, but when you get older, and you really like a boy, sometimes you'll do stupid things to try to get him to like you back."

"I hope not."

"You say that now, but you probably will. Sometimes, it's just hard to understand what some guys see in the girls they date."

"What don't you get about Josh liking Allie?"

"Well, for one, she's not as pretty as either Cecilia or me. Two, she's so shy and quiet!"

I try to process this.

"It seems to me that the people who should date are people who both naturally really like each other. Can you really convince someone who doesn't like you that way to, well, like you that way?"

"I think so," Vittoria replies defensively. "Sometimes, boys don't notice you unless you put yourself out there, like flirt with them."

"If what Cecilia did last night is flirting, I don't think it works."

"THAT wasn't flirting; it was . . . I don't know what it was."

"Stupid? I can't imagine Josh likes Cecilia more now than he did before the movies last night. In fact, I know he doesn't."

Vittoria pauses. "Like I said, some things will seem funny or cool at the moment but actually aren't."

I slowly nod my head.

"Did you really think it was funny?"

"For a second, it did seem funny and shocking, you know? I just couldn't believe it. But then I just felt worse and worse afterward."

"Vittoria, you're so pretty, and I've watched guys stare at you. You could have any single guy you want. But instead, you want one who's taken, which means he's not into you. That doesn't make any sense!"

"Of course you would think that!" she snaps. Her reaction surprises me. And then, softer, she offers, "Of course that's what you would see."

"Am I wrong?!" I push back.

"Pretty much. Maybe guys look at me but finding a guy who really wants to get to *know* me, that's hard. I know I'm pretty, and guys like to look at me. But because of that, it can feel like I'm a piece of meat. Girls get easily jealous and are mean to me. Shelly Diaz told Cecilia that she doesn't want to hang out with me anymore when she's with Malcolm because she's seen him look at me, and she's afraid I'll steal him from her. I'm not even interested in Malcolm! And since we all hang out together when we go to the mall or the movies, now I'm not invited if Shelly and Malcolm will be there. I feel like an outcast."

How could anyone complain about being pretty? I wonder. But I also think my sister is letting me into a world I know nothing about, and my curiosity gets the better of me. I want to know more.

"Serah, girls can be really mean and petty."

"I already know *that*."

"Well, I wish I could say it gets easier, but it gets worse. There is so much drama. Girls say one thing to your face and then, in the next second, whisper the opposite behind your back. They'll cause fights just to have something to talk about. They try to get friends to take sides in fights that aren't even theirs. And if you're popular and guys like you, then you're a target. So people say mean things about me all the time. I have had plenty of boys tell me they're interested in me, but none of them really get to *know* me."

"Why would you need to have a boyfriend to begin with?"

"I don't *need* to have a boyfriend," she mocks my tone, "but it is nice to have guys pay attention to you. I don't think you can understand yet. It can be fun!"

"So can getting good grades, spending time doing what you love, sports, service, reading—"

"Like *National Geographic*?" she interrupts.

"Obviously," I smile back.

"I don't know. Honestly, I've never had a real *boyfriend*, just crushes—guys who've liked me or who I've liked. Like I said, when it comes down to it, most of the time, it's obvious a guy just wants to be able to tell his friends he made out with me."

"Ew."

"I'm just being honest."

"Well, if I'm being honest, I think Cecilia sucks, and you should find some new friends."

"It's not that easy to just 'make new friends.' So many girls are already in groups, and it can be hard to move from one to another."

"Well, I think you should try. Because I know you, and I know there's *so much more* to you than trying to get guys to notice you. You're a very good singer and dancer; you're so creative, and I think you're a really good writer."

"When have you read my writing?" she questions, tilting her head in confusion.

"Well, your diary, for one. I also go through the pockets of your dirty pants in the laundry room and find all sorts of notes . . ."

"SERAH! Are you serious?!"

"No!" I laugh. "You're so gullible, just like Mom. No, I've read some of your school papers though."

"You're not funny. How?"

"In your notebooks in your backpack."

"Really?"

"Yeah, I have. I really liked your short story for language arts about the ballerina."

"Well, that's . . . good, I guess. 'Cause I don't think I have a future in dance."

"Why not?"

"I don't have the right 'physique,'" she says, making air quotes. "I'm too curvy—everywhere."

"Um, I think you've been looking at too many of those magazines you read. You know, the ones where if you flip through the pages, no one looks real, and nearly every pic is of someone who's super skinny?"

"Ha, I know what you mean, but no, it's not because of that. I wish it were."

"How could your curves mean you can't dance?"

"You wouldn't understand. Ballet dancers all look the same, kind of like the Rockettes in New York. Did you know to be a Rockette, you have to be between five foot six and five foot ten and a half inches tall?"

"I had no idea. Why do you even know that?"

"Because I thought I wanted to be one. But I don't think I could be. I'm only five foot two right now, and the chances of me growing four or more inches are slim."

I'm only an inch shorter than Vittoria, which I hadn't really thought about before now. I realize I will most likely end up taller than she is.

"It could happen."

"But probably not. My point is that no matter how much I try to prevent myself from getting curvier or make myself taller, I can't change that. I keep trying to watch my diet to make sure I don't get too big, but almost all the dancers in my class are thinner than I am."

"If you want to grow, I would think you need to eat more, not less." She smiles condescendingly like she knows something I don't. "If you want to be a regular dancer, like, not a Rockette, would you still have to be five foot six?"

"No, it depends on the dance company. I think Mom just discourages me from going for it because she knows what a tough life it can be. And then she says, 'Vittoria, you don't have a dancer's body.'" Her imitation of our mom is spot-on.

"I know Mom means well, but sometimes, when she's trying to be helpful, she seems . . ." I trail off.

"Critical?" Vittoria finishes my sentence.

"Yeah."

"I know." We sit and say nothing for a moment. "Why don't we get to this face washing?"

I nod.

"I read in a beauty magazine that you start with luke-warm or warm water. A little warmth will help open up your pores." After turning on the hot water tap and then the cold, she cups her hands under the running water and splashes her face from the bottom up. "When I wash, I rub circles in an upward motion when putting the soap on and then rinse."

"Why do you go in circles like that? What difference does it make?"

"I don't know, but Mom told me to do that, so I always have." Now her eyes are closed and squinty, and she rubs the lather all over, including on her eyes. She turns her head toward me with her eyes closed.

"Make sure you get everywhere, then rinse with cold water like this." Again, she splashes water from her cupped hands onto her neck and face to get all the soap off. She opens one eye to examine her face in the mirror, making sure all the soap is gone.

"Then, and Mom's the one who told me this, once you're done, get a clean, fresh towel and dab your face dry. Too much rubbing isn't good for it. You can also use a clean washcloth to wash your face, but I prefer using my hands. It's pretty simple, really. Now you try, and then we can put moisturizer on together."

I start running a little hot and a little cold water into the tap in my sink, and I have Vittoria check the temperature for me. I dab and splash water everywhere, decide to try the sample of Cetaphil, and begin washing like I would have done with a bar of soap in the shower before now. I turn the hot water tap off and start rinsing with the cold.

"That looks good, Serah. Just remember to wash your neck, too, next time."

"Oh, right," I say with my eyes closed, water dripping down my chin as I finish and turn off the faucet. I grab a clean hand towel and begin dabbing as I turn toward my sister.

"Now comes moisturizing, which is also pretty simple. I usually need two squirts from my pump, so here's how much that is."

I sift through my samples and find a matching Cetaphil moisturizer, dumping out what looks to be the same amount into my palm.

"I like to dab a spot of it on my chin, here on each cheek, my nose, two dabs on my forehead, and then I start on my neck with what's left in my hand and work my way up my face."

I follow her lead and begin at my neck, then rub the dabs of moisturizer on the various parts of my face into my skin until I can't see it anymore. I examine myself in the mirror and see that it's all rubbed in, and my skin looks fresh and a little shiny.

"Vittoria?"

"Yep?"

"Did you get zits before you got boobs?"

She laughs a little and thinks. "I can't really remember . . . I think they both started around the same time."

"Did your breasts hurt before they grew?"

"Oh, yeah, definitely. They also hurt *while* they grow. Mine haven't stopped hurting, especially when I have my period."

"Great. That sounds fun." I pause. "I don't understand why my face would start puberty before my breasts."

Now she laughs a little harder. I guess it is kind of silly. "Serah, they *will* grow. There's just no way to know *when*."

"I guess I could say the same thing about you."

"In what way?"

"You can be a dancer if you want to be. I know you can do it. You're a natural. If you keep practicing, you could be in the American Ballet Company or whatever that place in New York is. And even a Rockette."

My sister laughs. "It's American Ballet Theatre," she corrects me. "And thanks, little sis. Sometimes, you're not so bad."

Chapter 10:
MEAN BOYS

"Beautiful Soul"
—JESSE MCCARTNEY

In a way that's unique from everything else in all creation, like the Grand Canyon, a sitting lion, a soaring eagle—you, right where you are sitting, are a reflection of the beauty of God.
—DAVID PLATT

Spring comes in full force by May. At this point, the daffodils and tulips and cherry trees are done, the trees have leaves or are almost done sprouting them, and the grass is its gorgeous green. This month, for me, is soccer heaven.

What's not heaven is the really stupid drama. Vittoria told me girls get meaner, but what I wasn't prepared for was boys becoming jerks. It all started in the fall when some of the popular kids began a "group chat." I already told you that I feel like the only person in my class without an actual phone. So most of the people on the group chat have phone numbers, but a few—like me—have email addresses we can use for texting. Well, Veruca's minions, Regina and Gretchen, started the chat with Jed, and then they invited others, who invited more, and soon there were twenty-five people on one text chain. It got to be too much to read and keep up with, not to mention full of a lot of random gifs, emojis, and memes I didn't care about, so I left the group. But Courtney told me a few days ago that she wanted me to be back on it, so she added me. That was a big mistake.

Within a couple of hours, some of the boys had taken my email address and begun new group chats with just me. Well, not so much "chats" because they were one-sided. The first one was just a silly prank where two boys tried to convince me that my parents were getting deported for being foreigners. I knew that was a joke, so I ignored it. But then some of the boys started sending mean messages.

> Ur poop
> Pooop pooooooooooooop
> U smell like poop

I'm pretty sure that was Nick, but he's not in my contacts, and he has an actual phone number, so I can't tell who it is. And then I got this message yesterday.

> U suck
> U have no life

Ur poop
U eat poop

Who is this?

No answer. I decided to ignore it. But I had no idea who had sent them. I came to school today feeling like I was moving on, just letting it go. But as I was adding water to my water bottle at the fountain just around the corner from some of the boys' lockers, I heard Nick and Seth Rodriguez talking about me and the *funny* texts they had sent!

Seth. My crush. Was crushing me. Not crushing *on* me but being a total jerk. And he thought it was *funny*. Tears welled up in my eyes, and I ran to the bathroom to find a safe place to cry. It made me late for class, which I hate, and I think it was obvious that I had been crying. I barely made it through my morning classes.

Now that it's lunchtime, I'm heading to see Mrs. Caldwell. I let a lot of time go by since I last went to see her. She did say to come back anytime, and now is as good a time as any. I head to the guidance department and ask if she's there.

"She is, honey; I think she is just eating lunch at her desk. Go ahead and go back and knock," Mrs. Swofford offers.

I head down the hallway and find her door cracked about six inches. I knock, causing the door to push in about another six inches as Mrs. Caldwell says while swallowing, "Come in."

"Hi, Mrs. Caldwell."

"Oh, Serah, HI!" She lights up, genuinely happy to see me. "It's been a while. How have you been?"

"I've been good. Busy with homework and soccer. I'm sure you know," I say, feeling a little guilty that I haven't been back before now. I had meant to return to do more research.

"I *do* know. In fact, I was busy running around in many different directions at your age too. It's good to slow down sometimes though. What can I do for you?"

"I kind of, well, I don't know. I just wanted to say hello and touch base." I fill the air with a bunch of small talk about life. She asks me some questions, and I give her the cookie-cutter answers. Then I am brave enough to start the real conversation. "Some things have happened since I was here a few weeks ago. I had an interesting conversation with my sister." I decide to start there.

"Oh, really? Do sit down. Did you bring your lunch? Clearly, I don't mind if you eat in here." She motions at one of the two chairs across from her desk with her hand that's not holding a sandwich. I pick the chair on the right and sit upright, keeping my back straight. I'm not sure how long I'm going to be here, but I don't want to seem like I'm too comfortable either. I unwrap my sandwich.

"What was interesting about your conversation?"

"Well, you know Vittoria, right?"

"I do."

"And she's really pretty, right?"

"Well, I guess that's subjective to a large extent, but I find her to be very pretty."

"Yeah, so do I. Well, it turns out there are struggles to being really pretty too."

"Oh, really?" She cocks her head to one side as if to say, *Do tell*.

"Well, apparently, it feels like boys want to date her, but she said they don't really want to *get to know* her. Like, the real her. The person she is inside."

"What do you think about that?"

"Honestly, she sounded lonely. It was believable. On the other hand, it's kind of hard to feel bad for her."

"It is often very hard to see someone's struggles when looking from the outside. But we all have them," she says, then takes a deep breath. I wonder what Mrs. Caldwell's struggles are and if they have anything to do with her scar.

"Serah, some people work very hard to have an outward beauty that draws us to them, makes us stop and look, or even stare. And it's easy to see that and desire that as well. But comparison can make us miserable. It's like chasing the wind. And if your ultimate goal is to look good, it's a shallow one. It's like a puddle." She looks out the window, takes a bite of her sandwich, and chews while I wait for her to continue. Then she looks back at me, into my eyes, and locks them there. "You, my dear, are not a puddle. You are a pristine river with deep waters that are hiding gemstones at the bottom. And I bet some of the most alluringly beautiful people wish those who stare at the surface would look past the puddle. We all have hidden treasures below. Vittoria, you, your friends—everyone."

"I never thought of it like that," I manage. If I'm a river, she's an ocean. "I think Vittoria has a lot of friends who look at the puddles. I can tell maybe she doesn't really even like the friends she has. This one friend, Cecilia, came over, and they did something really mean."

"Do you want to tell me about it?"

I slump into my chair, making myself comfortable, set my lunch down, and begin relaying the whole story as I know it about what happened at the movies with Josh, Allie, Cecilia, and Vittoria. Mrs. Caldwell listens intently. I then tell her about the sleepover, my soccer game, and Vittoria telling me she apologized to Josh.

"Does Vittoria have other friends who come over that you like?"

"Yeah, I think some of them are nice and kind."

"That's good. Middle school is really, really hard. I don't know a single middle school girl who hasn't had to deal with 'mean girl' behavior, who hasn't been through something like Cecilia and Vittoria did to Allie. I wish I had better news. Kids, especially girls, but boys as well, can be so mean sometimes."

Of *course,* the text messages come to my mind immediately. I look out the window, trying to eat a few bites of my sandwich as a distraction, but I put it down, and my eyes start to water despite all my effort to keep it from happening.

"Are you okay, Serah? What's wrong?"

As she hands me a tissue, I think to myself that I'm glad she asked. The more I am open with her, the closer I get to finding out how she seems so comfortable with herself, seemingly unaware of that huge scar on her face.

"No, no, I'm okay. I sort of had my first real crush until this morning. But it turns out he's a jerk."

I have my iPod on me, so I show her the texts. It's easier than having to read them out loud to her and relive them.

She sits back in her chair when she's done and doesn't speak for a minute.

"The one set of texts is from my crush."

We both let that sit in the air for a bit.

"Oh, Serah, I'm so, so sorry these boys did this. Group texts can start off harmless but often turn into a real problem, even a school problem. Believe me when I say I'm not in any way trying to minimize how hurtful these must be or excuse the behavior. But I do think that sometimes kids, and especially boys your age, do things like this to be funny. What they don't realize is that most people don't think it's funny. And often boys do things like this to the girls that they *like*, not the ones they *don't* like. But usually, with sixth-grade boys, it's the former. In other words, they're trying to be funny."

"That makes no sense at all."

"It doesn't have to make sense. It just is what it is."

"It kind of sucks," I say.

"Stinks. It stinks," she corrects me.

96

"Stinks."

"Is Seth your first crush?"

I have to think about this. He's actually not. I sort of liked a boy all the way back in first grade, but he tried to get me to lick the floor, and I realized he was an idiot. Then, last year, I sort of liked Nick, but I got over that. Now Courtney's the one who likes him.

"Not really."

"Did the other one go away?"

"Yes, actually. Both of them," I say pensively. "I guess I didn't make them go away; they just did. And, like I said, my crush on Seth is over. I think."

"Crushes come and go. Sometimes, the feelings can seem so intense and true in the moment, but it's amazing that even a day, a week, or a month later, the feelings are gone. And you will find yourself crushing on someone new. Sometimes, your crush does something to turn you off, like picks his nose and eats it in plain view, or, in this case, he sends you some mean texts. Other times, the feelings just wear off. It's a good thing to remember that as it's happening so you don't get so wrapped up in it."

"Yeah, I guess so."

More silence. Then the class bell rings. I can't believe I've been in here for forty-five minutes.

"I could sit and chat with you forever, but I'm guessing you should get to class."

"Yeah, I should probably go," I hear myself say reluctantly. I've shared so many deep, private parts of myself; I don't really want to leave before asking about her scar. It seems fair—like I shared, and now I can get her to share. But I chicken out, and I begin packing up my stuff. After hurling my backpack over my shoulders, I grab the rest of my sandwich in one hand so I can eat it while I head to class. Mrs. Caldwell stops me as I turn to leave.

"What's still on your mind, Serah?"

"Well, just what you said about how growing up is hard no matter who you are. I'm thinking about Cecilia and Vittoria and me." *And you, Mrs. Caldwell.* But I'm still chicken. "Cecilia is just one of those girls who are really pretty on the outside, but she's just ugly and jealous and mean on the inside. I don't think she's beautiful at all."

"You know, Serah, that's a very interesting observation."

"It makes me wonder what made her like that."

"Who knows? You never know what someone's family life is like or what values a person is being taught. Maybe Cecilia has learned that love must be earned, and her good looks are how she will earn it."

"I guess."

"You are very fortunate to have a loving mother and father."

I don't respond. Mrs. Caldwell looks at me, raising one eyebrow at my non-reaction.

"Do you agree?"

"Oh, I know my parents love me," I say honestly. "They say it to me; they provide for me, and they sacrifice for me. It's just . . . sometimes, I wish they were a little different."

"Interesting." Pause. "Have you ever talked to either of them about some of the things you wish were different?"

"Nah," I say.

"Well, maybe one day you will. I think your mom would probably like to hear from you."

"Why do you care so much about me talking to my mom?"

She pauses. "In general, no matter how much we might think our moms are the last people we can relate to, they do know what it's like to be a girl growing up, and they care more about us than perhaps anyone else."

"Sometimes, I don't like the way she shows that she cares."

"I don't know this for a fact, but I think every daughter has felt that way about her mother at some time or another."

At that moment, the late bell rings.

"I should go," I say. Next time. I'll ask her next time. Mrs. Caldwell hesitates for a second too.

"Sounds good. It was so nice to see you, Serah, and I thoroughly enjoyed our visit."

"Me, too, Mrs. Caldwell," I say as I head out the door. While walking down the hallway, I can't figure out what it was, but something was different at the end of our conversation. Like, it seems that Mrs. Caldwell also didn't share something that was on her mind. I shake it off, figuring it's nothing.

I am convinced she and Rachel, Plain and Large are similar. I make a mental note to add Mrs. Caldwell to the

Beautiful List. And I promise myself that I'm going to ask her about her scar the next time I see her.

If only I knew under what circumstances that would be.

Chapter 11:
CAN'T FIX IT ALL

"In My Daughter's Eyes"

—MARTINA MCBRIDE

His name was Nabal and his wife's name was Abigail.
She was an intelligent and beautiful woman.

—1 SAMUEL 25:3, EMPHASIS ADDED

There's one more appointment I have scheduled before school gets out for summer in June. It's with the orthodontist.

I love my orthodontist, Dr. Teryl. She is funny at the right times. She tries to make you laugh, but not when she has her hands in your mouth. It always drives me crazy when I'm at the dentist, and he asks me questions right as he puts his fingers, little mirrors or picks in my mouth *as if* I can answer him.

I spent all of fourth grade with a palate expander on the roof of my mouth because I had something called a crossbite. Now that I've nearly lost all my baby teeth, I'm going back in to see if I'm ready for braces.

The other thing I love about Dr. Teryl is that she sings in the office. Like, out loud. Really loudly.

I'm in the chair, waiting for her to examine my mouth. My mom is busy looking down at her phone, probably dealing with something about work while she's away from the office. I'm holding up my *National Geographic* so it covers the really bright light dangling above my face. They warn you it will seriously blind you if you stare at it, like the sun. So I'm productively killing two birds with one stone.

The sound of singing gets closer, and I think she might be headed to my chair. My arms are getting tired, lying here holding my magazine in midair.

Dr. Teryl plops into the seat behind my head and spins herself toward me, finishing the chorus of T. Swift's "Shake It Off" before addressing me.

"SERAH!" she almost yells. "How ARE you, kiddo?"

"I'm good!" I say, trying to match her enthusiasm.

"What are you, running Microsoft now? Graduating college early at age seventeen?"

"I just turned twelve on February 23."

"Ah, close enough. It won't be long. Let's take a look at those pearly whites." She hums along with the end of the song while I open wide. She starts using her little pick tool, digging into the caverns of my back teeth and tapping. There are few people who can get this close to your face while poking around in your mouth and still make you comfortable. I wonder, with how disgusting breath can smell and how gross mouths seem in general, why anyone would want to kiss with their lips open and roll their tongues around together. It sounds slimy and slobbery and legit disgusting.

"So are you brushing twice a day, flossing, and all that jazz, yadda yadda yadda?" She acts bored. Dr. Teryl is also awesome because *as* she's asking this question, she *removes her fingers from my mouth* so I can talk.

"Should I give you the answer you want to hear or the real answer?"

"Lie to me."

"Yes, I floss every night and brush twice a day religiously."

"Atta girl. I think what's happened, then, is the ONE OR TWO TIMES you forgot, a whole three-to-six months of plaque and tartar built up on your teeth." She gives me the old one eyebrow lift. "Haters are going to hate, Serah. And I HATE plaque. Have we had this talk before?"

"Yes, Dr. Teryl," I huff.

"So I don't have to tell you again that plaque is bacteria, and they eat leftover food in your mouth and then poop and pee on your teeth. You know that, right? There are three-to-six months of bacterial poop on your teeth."

"Well, when you put it *that* way," I say with a disgusted look on my face. "Okay, I'll brush more. And better. Honestly, I'm supposed to start washing my face now, too, so let's just add it to my already long to-do list for the morning and night."

"It's hard being a tenth-grader, I know."

"Sixth-grader."

"Whatever. Open wide, K?"

I do as I'm told.

"Stick out your tongue." She wraps some gauze around it and pulls it to the right, then the left. Then she puts her fingers on my face near my ears and tells me to open and shut several times.

"Okay, here's the deal." She motions for my mom to come over. "Your crossbite is completely fixed, and I'm not concerned about it coming back. We're just about to that place where we can put braces on to straighten everything out and help improve your bite. But I want to wait a little for two reasons: one, for you to grow some more. Even though your brain is about twenty, your jaw still has a *teeny* bit more growing to do and a few more baby teeth to donate to the tooth fairy. Only then will putting on braces make sense both physics-ly and physically." I roll my eyes. "Two, I want you to have some time to develop really great brushing and flossing habits because when the braces go on, OH MY, the plaque and tartar build up really fast, and it's harder to brush AND floss well." I give an even bigger eye roll. "And three . . ."

"You said there were two reasons."

"Right, two reasons. And three, so you can experience middle school as every kid should."

"You make it sound really fun."

"It's a rite of passage. We'll *make* it fun. You can pick colors for your elastics that go around the brackets, and . . . no, that's really the only fun part. Who am I kidding?"

"Every twelve-year-old's dream," I say.

"I knew you'd get it."

"Dr. Teryl?"

"Yes, Xena, Warrior Princess?"

"Before I get them on, can you be honest with me about how long it's going to take and exactly what to expect?"

"Sure. But let's do that at our next appointment. I don't want you worrying needlessly about it for the next six months."

"Thanks for that."

"Consider it my summer gift to you."

"See you in six months!"

She sings me out of the chair with the chorus of "So Long, Farewell" from *The Sound of Music*.

◦ ❈ ◦

Back in the car, I figure now is as good a time as any to try to talk to my mom. I've been dreading this conversation for weeks, trying to find exactly the right time for it. But in research, you go where the evidence takes you. I knew I would *eventually* have to talk to her. Three times now—two from Mrs. Caldwell and one from a fortune cookie—I've been encouraged to talk to my mom. Sometimes, evidence is scientific, and sometimes, you trust your gut—or God, or signs, or whatever you want to call them. Besides, Mrs. Caldwell made a good point: She *is* my *mom*. Maybe she will have something wise to say.

"Mom?"

"Yes, dear."

I start with a question I've been wondering about for a while. "Are you disappointed in me?"

"What? No! What do you mean?" she tries to look at me but has to keep her eyes on the road.

"Just, am I a disappointment?"

"Sweetheart, you could never 'be a disappointment.' You're my daughter, and I love you with everything I've got. You know that, right?"

"Well, yes," I say hesitantly, wondering if I can really explore this with her. I don't want to hurt her, but I am compelled by something more powerful than my fear of the answer that might come: a desire for the truth.

"But . . ." She lets the word linger because she knows there's more.

"Well, I was talking to Mrs. Caldwell at school, and, well . . . never mind." I don't think I can do it.

"Sweetheart, you know you can always tell me anything."

"Am I beautiful?" I blurt out.

"Of course you're beautiful!" She pulls up to a light and looks genuinely concerned. "You know you're beautiful, don't you? I tell you that a lot, don't I?"

"Mm-hmm," I say thoughtfully, the way you reply when there's more you have to say, but you're not saying it. She starts driving again.

"Well, why would you ask that, then?"

The river that's held by my mental dam breaks through and comes gushing forth. I choke out the next sentences through tears.

"Because some boys at school sent me messages this weekend telling me I'm ugly. Because I have zits popping up on my face that you take me to a dermatologist for, and I have crooked teeth that the orthodontist is going to fix, and I'm skinny, and my legs look like twigs, but I don't think there's a doctor for that." I pause, wondering for a minute if there actually *is* a doctor for that. I press on like the Hoover Dam has exploded. "You have told me many times that I inherited the Reynolds legs that 'have no shape.' I guess I'm not sure that fixing things about the way I look will ever make me beautiful, will ever be *enough*."

My mom looks a little stunned. Speechless, even.

"If my teeth are straight, and my zits go away, my face still won't be as pretty as yours or Vittoria's, and I'll still have twigs for legs. So maybe you *say* I'm beautiful, but do you really *mean* it?"

"Oh, sweetheart," my mom answers, with a shaky voice, on the verge of tears herself, "you are beautiful just the way you are."

"But HOW?" I wonder out loud. "How can I know that? How can I believe that despite all of my flaws?"

"Because we *all* have flaws. Every single one of us, sweetie. Some of them we can fix, some of them we can't. Beauty isn't just about what's on the outside. Beauty comes from within. You have the sweetest heart; you are caring; you treat others kindly, and you are the smartest kid I've ever met. Honestly."

I understand what she is saying to me, but her words ring hollow. I want so badly to believe her when she says I'm beautiful *just the way I am* because I can tell this is it. I'm either going to know this in my bones, or I'm not. And if I can't believe it when my mom says it, I can't imagine anyone else will be able to convince me. A thought comes to mind.

"Mom, what if I don't want to be smart? What if I *just* want to be beautiful?"

My mom pauses, takes a deep breath, and exhales, looking confused. "Why can't you be both?"

That's the million-dollar question, isn't it?

I try to think of a man who represents both brains and good looks and decide perhaps the athletes at Stanford or Harvard would fit that description. But an NFL quarterback? Or Ronaldo or Beckham or Messi? Or Lebron or Durant? They are, first and foremost, athletes. But maybe some of them are really smart or artistic or business-minded or sensitive or emotional or generous or kind. Maybe they wish they were known more for some of the other things about them that have nothing to do with their game.

And women—I try to think of some who represent both brains and beauty. I think of Ruth Bader Ginsberg (God rest her soul!), Jane Goodall, and Emma Watson. No offense to our most famous female Supreme Court justice or primatologist and anthropologist ever, but only one of those three makes me think "beautiful." (Though to be fair, RBG recently died in her old age, and Jane is in her eighties. In their old photos, they both look pretty.)

Of course, I say none of this out loud. We pull into our driveway, and she stops short of the garage. Instead of sharing, I simply reply, "I don't know, Mom. Can I?" We both let the heavy silence sit. I can tell my mom is thinking through her next words carefully.

"I am so sorry some boys called you ugly. Shame on them. YOU are NOT ugly. You are beautiful, *and* you are wicked smart. What can I do to help you believe you are *both*?"

I sit quietly, thinking, *Well, Mom, you've had two plastic surgeries that I know about. You get Botox and something called filler injections. You get dressed up and put on makeup to go to the gym. You stand in front of your mirror and talk about how you need to lose this and change that.*

Here goes. I turn toward her, and in the faintest voice I have above a whisper, I utter genuinely, "Believe it about yourself." And my mom's river—which I think she has a dam for too—breaks. And she hugs me as tears stream down her face, caressing my back, saying nothing and everything at the same time.

Chapter 12:

DRAMA, DRAMA

"Headspace"

—RILEY CLEMMONS

The in-between is just as important as the destination.
Stay the course . . . you are a beautiful work of art!

—JAIME JAMGOCHIAN, INSTAGRAM ACCOUNT

I'm studying my Beautiful List at my desk, listening to birds chirping outside my window. It takes very little thought before I decide they deserve to be in the left column.

I've just added my grandmothers and all my close friends to the list. My grandmothers are both wrinkly and old, but they are most definitely beautiful. I've added Emma Watson, Jane Goodall, and RBG. The very fact that my grandmas and the last two make the list is proof that beauty is not about age. I'm not trying to get too deep here, but it seems like everyone who loves me can say without a doubt that I'm beautiful. And vice versa. I didn't hesitate to put my mom, Vittoria, and Courtney on the Beautiful List when I first made it. For various qualities, such as strength, patience, grace, wisdom, kindness, and appearance, I can put all of the important females in my life on the Beautiful List. All of them except for myself.

Why do I hesitate when it comes to me? Am I simply being harder on myself than I am on others? And if that's the case, do *all* girls do this? Or *most*? Is it because we don't think we deserve to be beautiful? Does *every* girl have to go through this? Or just some of us? How many women know they are beautiful—not just to *look at* but just know in their core that they are plainly and simply beautiful?

I must know people who know they're beautiful. I think Mrs. Caldwell would put her own name on the list. I'm going to ask her to make sure, right after I ask her about her scar, but I think she would. Rachel would definitely put her name on it. I knew her for five minutes, and I'm more sure of this than of global climate change. Maybe it's easier for girls to believe they're beautiful when they're seven. But I'm not sure the seven-year-old version of myself would have put my name on the Beautiful List either. And I have two parents who love me and give me everything I need and more. What about the girl who is poor or, worse, unwanted or ignored? Does she even *think* about beauty?

I head downstairs to eat breakfast while my brain continues to chew on this mystery. My brother's going to take me to school, while my mom takes Vittoria because she has an eye appointment this morning.

I notice my mom's eyes look a little puffy, and she's not wearing makeup. She's also in the most "mom" clothes I've ever seen her wear. But she seems otherwise okay.

"Good morning, gorgeous," she says, smiling at me. It seems like this is some "new her" emerging from a chrysalis like a butterfly, probably because of our conversation yesterday. Or maybe I'm reading into things too much.

"Good morning. What's for breakfast?"

"Whatever you're making." She grins, cupping her coffee between her two hands like she's hugging it because it's so lovable.

"Cereal. It's the breakfast of champions."

"I'd love some!" She's a little too energetic and eager. We eat our muesli in silence. It's kind of funny because she doesn't like muesli. It feels like she's trying to bond with me in some way, but she doesn't know how to do it.

"Serah-boo, you ready? I need to get to school a few minutes early," Alessandro asks as he opens the fridge to grab some cold pizza he will probably eat while driving. That seems gross. And totally safe. #eyeroll

"I can be fast, but why?"

"Knock-knock."

"Ugh, I hate your knock-knock jokes. Who's there?"

"Nunya."

I go through the motions. "Nunya who?"

"Nunya business. Let's go!"

"I need to finish my muesli," I manage to get out while I chew the cereal in my mouth.

"Hurry up!" he says, his tone annoyed. I decide not to say that maybe he should have given me more warning. I finish quickly and start putting my backpack together.

"Have a good day, sweetheart," my mom says as she comes over to give me a hug goodbye. It feels nice.

"Bye, Mom. You too."

◎ ❀ ◎

It's a Wednesday, which means I have PE. Because it's late spring, we've begun our four-week swimming unit, which means we *all* have to get into swimsuits.

You already know how I feel about swimsuits. Now, I have to wear one in front of *half the boys in my class*. Why don't Speedos come with a pad built in so you can't see nipples through them? (Not a maxi pad—ew—but like a liner, like my mom's bathing suits have in the chest area.) I should write them a letter.

Dear Speedo,

No twelve-year-old girl should have to flaunt her non-existent (or growing) torpedo nipples to middle-school-aged boys at the pool. Please sew a liner or a pad of some sort into your PE suits.

Sincerely,
Still-in-Stage-One Serah

And even before the boys see all the girls in their see-through Speedos, the girls have to get dressed in the locker room. It's one thing to strip down to bras and panties for regular PE. Now Mandy King gets a whole new way to victimize us.

Getting completely naked also makes it super obvious which girls have started shaving their legs and armpits. Mandy King was the first one I knew of (of course) back in early fifth grade. But it turns out that some of the girls with dark hair started in fourth. I think I'm one of the last ones left who hasn't started shaving at least something. It makes me feel a little pressured to start. My mom says to wait longer because it's a pain, and you can't stop once you start. Apparently, your hair grows back darker and thicker when you start shaving. The last thing I want to do is make my legs look hairier or darker. I don't want to draw any more attention to them or make them look any skinnier. But maybe if I start shaving the few strands of armpit hair I have, I won't smell as bad when I sweat.

Also, a man must have designed our locker room. Because there is only one changing stall in here, and Sonya Chen is *always* in it. If she's in your PE class, you know she's going to find a way to be the first one in the locker room so she can race over to it, hide behind the curtain, and be safe from everyone's eyes until she has wrapped herself in her towel like a burrito, a tortilla shell of privacy she sheds poolside just before jumping in. Of course, Veruca has yelled out loud right outside the changing stall curtain, "Why are you always in there, Sonya? What are you hiding from the rest of us?" Sonya is smart enough not to respond.

Some girls turn their backs to everyone to change, even when wearing bras. Some girls act like it's no big deal and take the chance to gossip while they change, comfortable in bras and panties. But even they turn around when they put on swimsuits so all you can see is their butts.

And then there are the girls who don't mind getting completely naked in front of everyone. Jordan Fleming—the girl who first developed breasts in fourth grade—is one of those girls who was born to be naked, if there is such a thing. She just doesn't care. She also has the equivalent of a squirrel's tail worth of hair in her pubic area already, and I would say she's in stage three of breast development. Maybe she wouldn't flaunt her stuff so much if she weren't almost done maturing. It's hard not to stare because she puts it all out there on display. It's as if she's saying, "Take a look, girls; this is where you're headed." She's a roadmap for those who don't have older sisters. Jordan is the only girl who Veruca doesn't terrorize on this subject.

When changing, I prefer to keep my underpants and bra on at all times. If I have to strip all the way down, like today, I put my bathing suit on *over* my underwear and then remove them. You can leave your underpants on, pull one side of them as hard as they will stretch, and pull that leg all the way out, then pull the underpants out the *other* leg of the bathing suit and never get naked. I do the same thing with my bra once the top half of my swimsuit is on. This is definitely the way to go in a locker room without being singled out for "hiding" behind a door or a curtain but also shielding your girly parts from view.

Today, I am a little nervous about how swimming will go because Olivia and Jessica are in my PE class. Sometimes, I feel like I'm stuck in the middle because I'm the only friend each of them has in PE. It can be a lot of pressure, especially when we have to break into groups of two for activities. Once Jessica was mad at me because I paired twice-in-a-row with Liv. I tried to explain to Jessica that I get to be with her all day in class, but this is the only class I have with Liv. She eventually got over it, but I have to remember to take turns to keep everyone happy.

Today, Coach wants us to swim laps in groups of three, and Jessica and I are assigned to the same lane based on swimming ability. The air outside is a little cold, and I can feel my nipples becoming hard and sticking out. I'm grateful to have my lane assignment, so I can jump in the heated water to hide them. Liv, who's a really good swimmer, asks if she can swim in our lane. Coach says fine and then gives us all instructions.

We're supposed to swim in a circle, like the way traffic goes on the street, as well as space ourselves out fifteen seconds apart, doing four-by-fifties in eight minutes. We do rock-paper-scissors to see who starts off, and I lose, so I go first. Jess is second and Liv third. I start, get back to the wall, and realize I have a forty-five-second rest. When I look up the lane, Liv is literally hitting Jess's feet as she swims on her heels. She swims around her in the final ten yards, both arriving at the wall about the same time.

"What the heck?!" Jessica yells when she and Liv get to the wall.

"If you weren't so SLOW, I wouldn't have to go around you!" Liv shoots back.

"Why did you ask to be in this lane, then? If you're so good, you should swim in one of the faster lanes!" Jessica counters.

"Because I'd rather swim with my friend!" Liv squints her eyes at Jess, making it clear she said *friend* and not *friends*.

"Okay, okay, why don't you both calm down?" I try to referee.

"Are you taking her side?" Jessica shrieks.

"No, I'm not taking anyone's side! I'm on the side of peace," I say.

"Well, if you were really a good friend, you'd take my side," Jessica says.

"That's not fair," I say calmly. I look at Liv. "Liv, if you just go first, we won't have this problem. I'll go second, and Jess can go third, okay?"

"Fine, as long as Jess is last because she sucks at swimming. Most nerds do," she scowls.

At this moment, Coach comes over because every other lane but ours has started its second fifty. The clock's at 2:10.

"Girls, is there a problem?"

"Nope, no problem here!" Liv says and pushes off the wall to start her fifty before Coach can ask her to move. Coach looks at the two of us, warning us with her eyes that we'd better shape up, and I push off the wall. When I get back, Jess is a good twenty seconds behind.

"She can be so sensitive!" Liv says to me about Jess.

I look at her and say nothing.

"Why are you looking at me like that? I didn't do anything wrong."

"Can we just swim?" I ask, sighing. Sometimes, there's no sense in getting in the middle or trying to help, especially before people have the chance to cool off and think.

Just as Jess hits the wall, Liv pushes off again.

"She is SO RUDE! Why wouldn't she just slow down for the last ten yards? Did she say anything to you?"

"Can we just drop it, Jess? I don't really want to be in the middle."

"Fine, but I know you heard her say 'friend,' and she said I suck at swimming and called me a nerd. She can be really mean."

Again, I say nothing. I'm grateful to have the excuse that the clock's now at 4:15, and I have to push off. While I swim, I wonder how I could possibly help make things right. Otherwise, the next four weeks of PE are going to be miserable. Maybe I'll ask Coach to keep us all in separate lanes.

I avoid both Jess and Liv in the locker room and change in silence. Luckily, Jess drops it when we get to social studies.

❀

The next time I see Liv, it's at soccer on Thursday. As I get out of the car and Alessandro reminds me that he's going to pick me up, I walk up to pre-practice gossip of Liv embellishing the pool lane story, calling Jessica more names. I wish I could avoid being sucked into this stupid drama altogether.

"She's *SO SLOW* that I try to go around her, and she literally sticks her left leg out to kick me as I swim by." Courtney waves hi without words, and I roll my eyes.

"What an idiot. Did you kick her back?" Katie asks.

"No, but I definitely yelled at her on the wall. Serah was there and saw the whole thing. I'm surprised I don't have a bruise."

Everyone looks at me like I'm supposed to say something or agree and empathize with Liv's retelling of the lap-swimming debacle of the year.

"Tell them, Serah," Liv says.

"Tell them what?" I reply impatiently.

"How mean Jessica the nerd was yesterday."

"I really don't want to get involved, and there's really no reason to talk about it *here*."

"So you're taking *her* side then, huh, Serah?"

"Like I said in the pool yesterday, I'm on the side of peace. And if you insist, the truth is I didn't see Jessica kick you. I'm not saying for sure that didn't happen, but I didn't see it. What I know is that you were purposely mean to her and called her a name."

"I did NOT!" Liv counters, her voice getting higher by the second. This is the second time in two days when

I wish a coach were nearby listening so I didn't have to be the adult.

"Who's telling the truth here?" Courtney puts us both on trial. I look at her in disbelief, shocked that she would possibly believe I had any reason to lie. I say nothing, just seethe in my head quietly.

"*Obviously,* you're going to believe Serah because she's your BFF. But I'm the victim here; Jessica kicked me, and Serah refused to back me up."

I can't believe we're supposedly talking about the same event. And I definitely don't want to ask Jessica if she kicked Liv because I just want this to go away. I know I didn't see it, but I guess that doesn't mean it didn't happen. But if it did, why didn't Liv say so yesterday?

"All I know is what I saw and heard, Liv, and I really don't want to get involved. Can we just drop it?"

"But what name did Liv call Jessica, Serah?" Courtney asks me. I plead at her with my eyes to just *stop*.

"She called her a nerd and said she sucked at swimming."

"I soooooooooooooo did not," Liv says, huffing and puffing.

"Alright, I'm dropping it," Courtney says. But I am unsure of whether she believes me. And at the same moment, Coach calls us over to start practice. So *of course* I am distracted. And I haven't even had the chance to talk to Courtney about my conversation with my mom yet. I'm definitely not going to do it now that things feel so off. I hate it when everything just feels so . . . wrong.

Especially between my friends. How could Courtney not believe me? When there's a disagreement like this, my mom has taught me that it always helps to think through who has more to gain by lying. I can't think of a single reason why I would lie about what happened. But I can think of a few why Liv would.

◎ ❀ ◎

I'm relieved when Alessandro pulls up to get me. I need a break from all the drama. It's so stupid to think all this began because Liz wanted to swim laps with me. And now we're not talking, and I feel like a ping-pong ball between Liv and Jess—not to mention Courtney has gotten dragged into this despite having nothing to do with it. This has been such a dramatic week.

"Hello? Is anybody home?" I hear, breaking into my train of thought.

"What?" I hear myself say.

"Did you hear anything I just said to you?" Alessandro asks.

"I can't say that I did."

"Mom said we should stop for food on the way home because she's grabbing something with Vittoria after dance. You okay with Pizza Brama?"

"Oh my gosh, yes, I forgot he was open again!"

"I'm going to get three pizzas. I'm not even kidding."

We pull up to a light.

"Do you need to look up the menu on my phone, or do you know what you want? Maybe you can call while we're driving and get the order started."

"I know what I want. What do you want?"

"Definitely a Wise Guy and a Pepperoni."

"That's only two pizzas, not three. And green light," I say.

"Grr, why do all girls seem to think guys need to be told when the light changes?"

Alessandro looks at me to show his frustration as he hits the gas. No sooner than we pull into the intersection do I hear honking while several other things seem to happen at once. I instinctively look toward the sound and see the front of a car no more than twenty feet away heading straight for us. The next thing I hear is the loudest sound I've ever heard, like an explosion. And then there's nothing. Pitch-black nothingness.

Chapter 13:
MISNOMER

"Scars to Your Beautiful"
—ALESSIA CARA

Self flashes off frame and face.
—GERARD MANLEY HOPKINS

"Oh, hi, beautiful. It's so good to see you awake."

I blink a few times. My right eye stays completely closed, but my left eye opens and shuts normally, and I can see the afternoon sun pouring in through a window I don't recognize. There's a ray of bright light streaking across a bland, cream-colored wall, just grazing the bottom of a TV that's hung near the ceiling. Beneath it, I make out a dry erase board with information about someone named Nurse Rivera and how to reach her. My fuzzy mind is telling me I must be in a hospital, and as I turn my head slightly to look where my mom's voice is coming from, my neck and entire body feel like one big bruise. As I try to think of where I was before this, I draw a blank.

"Mom, I . . ."

"Shhh, don't try to talk."

"No, I . . . I'm okay." I realize how parched I am, and my throat is both scratchy and dry. It feels a little like I have strep throat. I point to the water on my bedside tray table that is just out of reach. My mom understands, grabs the paper cup, and points the straw right at my lips so I can drink without moving. Ice water has never tasted so good.

"What day is it?" I croak. I sound like a frog.

"Friday."

"How long have I been asleep?"

"About eighteen hours. I've tried to stay awake so I could be sure I was up when you awoke, but I think I dozed in the middle of the night for a few hours."

"What happened?"

"Don't worry about that right now, sweetie. Just focus on resting and getting better. I just sent a note to your dad to let him know you were stirring. As soon as he gets out of surgery, he's going to come up to be here too."

It does hurt to talk. The right side of my face feels tight and swollen. And parts are numb.

"Mom, I'm hungry. Can you order me a mushroom pizza? From Pizza Brama? Will they deliver here?"

At this, my mom bursts into tears. I think they're happy tears, but I can't be sure. My head seems fuzzy, but I don't remember her loving pizza *that* much. And then something clicks in my head, some memory about Pizza Brama, but I can't quite pinpoint it.

"Yes, of course! You may have all the pizza you want," she laugh-cries.

I take another sip of water while she calls Alessandro to have him track down the food truck and bring us a mushroom pizza, my favorite. My throat still feels awful.

"Why does my throat hurt so bad?"

"It's probably because you're talking," she jokes as she wipes her face with some tissues and blows her nose.

"Mom?"

"Yes?"

"Can I ask you something?"

"You can ask me anything as long as it doesn't hurt."

Too late for that! My brain is waking up and feeling less fuzzy. "Did you know you misspelled my name?"

"Huh? What?"

"My name. The Italian way to spell Serafina is with an *f*."

"Oh, sweetheart, we didn't misspell it. Well, not really. What made you think we misspelled it?"

"Since I looked up what my name means and realized the way I spell it is Hebrew."

"Oh no! I wish you would have said something to me." My mom chokes back fresh tears. I'm not used to seeing her emotional, and this is *twice* in a couple of minutes. She fights through it.

"Let me tell you a little story. I think you'll like it, and it will rest your weary throat. When we found out we were pregnant with a third baby, we were elated. We already had a boy and a girl, so we decided to be surprised about your gender. We had some boy and girl names we liked, but we wanted to meet you before choosing. When you came out, rather quickly and with so much vigor, you didn't look like either Alessandro or Vittoria did when they were born. Your father and I both looked at you, and each of us saw a piece of ourselves. The name Serafina suited you so well."

She gazes toward the window—I think because she's remembering her first moments with me. I instantly wonder if I should have asked this question another time when I didn't feel so groggy and was more certain I would remember the details.

"At that moment," she continues, "your father, who had agreed that we could choose Italian names for all of you, suggested a compromise. He said, 'Elenore, I know we both love the name Serafina. My middle name is Philip, with a *ph*. Would you be willing to spell her name with a *ph*, after me?'"

My mom's gaze returns to me, misty-eyed with remembrance. "How could I possibly say no? It seemed to fit so perfectly. We gave you the Italian name we had chosen together, with an ode to your father's namesake. Plus, Sophia Loren—one of my favorite actresses, as you know—was born Sofia Scicolone, with an *f*, but changed it to *ph*. She clearly thought *ph* was better."

Of *course*—I had looked up the meaning of our cat's name before and found that Sophia means wisdom or skill, but the meaning is the same whether you spell it with an *f* or a *ph*. I wonder if Sofia Scicolone changed her name to sound less Italian. I'm jolted back to the conversation at hand when my mom starts talking.

"I guess we never said anything to you because it never came up. I should have known better with how smart you are. I'm so sorry we never told you."

A tear creeps out of each of my eyes as I realize my parents didn't make a mistake; my name wasn't a forgotten third child accident but a decision made out of both of their love. Part of me is mad at her for not telling me this before now. Another part of me is wondering why I never asked her about the spelling of my name instead of assuming two pretty smart people got it wrong.

The tear on my right cheek begins to burn me as it streaks down below my eye, and instinctively, I touch the area to wipe away the tear. I wince. Instead of finding smooth skin, I feel a tender wound that makes me pull back my hand, both in pain and fear. My mom was unable to stop me before it happened. Now, she's watching as I slowly and ever-so-gently dab my ring finger across what must be teeny tiny stitches stretching over at least a two-inch area along my cheekbone.

The mist that welled in her eyes while speaking of my birth is still there. It dawns on me that some of her emotion is because she can see me, and my face must look awful. As I begin to process what I'm feeling and touching, my dad walks in.

"There's my princess," he says with a warm smile. He's wearing his customary hospital scrubs and has a mask pulled down around his neck. He looks exhausted.

"Dad," I say, but he, too, motions me to be quiet, realizing he's walked into a room where two ladies are crying. Instead of entertaining the sorrow, he powers forward, like he's so good at doing.

"You are the strongest person I know," he says. "I have seen so many car accident victims who suffer far less severe injuries than you have and spend a week in the hospital. But we all think you can be released in two to three days."

I was in a car accident?

"What . . . happened? And what happened to my face? I don't remember anything."

My parents look at each other and share one of those glances where they decide something together without saying a word. I think they know they can't sugarcoat anything with me. At least, not anymore.

"Alessandro was bringing you home from soccer yesterday." I start to process, trying to remember my last thoughts from not even twenty-four hours ago. Do I even remember soccer? "When he started to drive through a green light at the intersection of Falls and River Roads, another driver heading north on Falls ran the red light and rammed into the front passenger side of the car. Because you were on the side that was hit, the glass in your window shattered, and your head hit the car frame, giving you a black eye and a concussion. Some of the shattered glass cut you in various places."

My dad cuts in to relieve my mom, who can barely hold it together. He trembles ever so slightly.

"The wounds on your arm, your neck, and your right cheek required stitches." My dad—*my dad*—is choking back tears. "It could have been so much worse. We're both so glad you're going to be okay."

A small part of me wonders if any of his emotion is because he thinks my face is ruined. I quickly remind myself not to believe the worst.

"Baby, your concussion is why you can't remember much about the accident and also why the doctors want to monitor you a couple more days," my mom says.

I steady myself to ask my next question. I am suddenly queasy and scared. "Am I going to be able to see out of my right eye?" This is my favorite eye, the one with heterochromia. I brace myself for the answer.

"Your eye should be fine, and everything should heal. You don't need to worry about anything. We had Dr. Klein sew up the wound on your face. You have forty-six microscopic stitches across your cheek—"

"Elenore, I'm not sure the details are helpful," my dad cuts in. "Serah-boo, aside from me, Dr. Klein is the best. You should barely have a scar when you have healed."

"But I'll have one." I let that sink in. Then I echo the good news: My eye is going to be okay. I'm not going to be one-eyed. I'm going to be able to see again on the right side. But my cheek—I process the idea of having a scar on my face and immediately think of Mrs., um, Mrs. What's-her-name—Caldstone?

"Will one of you give me a mirror? I want to see it."

My parents glance at each other again and share another silent conversation with just their eyes. Then they both look at me together.

"I'm not sure that's a good idea," my mom explains. "Your face has been through a trauma and will look much better tomorrow than it does today, and even better the day after that. Why don't you just wait until we get home? The lighting in here is awful too," she points toward the dull, fluorescent lights, trying to be somewhat lighthearted.

"Mom, I want to see what happened. I can handle it."

She glares at my dad for support, but he nudges her. Reluctantly, she gets the compact from her purse. She hands it over, and I feel like a freak show with the way they stare at me.

I hear a scream-shriek, very shrill and awful sounding, and then realize it's coming from me. I see my mouth open in the compact mirror, and no one else could possibly be making the noise. My mom's expression turns to one of agony, and she hits my dad in the shoulder as if to say, "I told you this wasn't a good idea." I stop screaming long enough to breathe in, but then these uncontrollable, short moans keep coming out, like a wounded animal or what a woman in labor sounds like in the movies. I am queasy all over again and fear I might throw up the water I just drank.

My face is somewhat exactly what I should have expected, based both on what my parents said and the stitches I felt, but also so very surreal to see. I swallow back the bile that tries to make its way up my throat and will myself not to upchuck. The entire right side of my face has bruising of various shades of purples, pinks, blues, greens, and yellow. The streak of stitches along my cheekbone runs from the edge of my temple in a slant down to about an inch from my nose. My eye is swollen shut, and the right side of my face is about twice as large as usual with puffiness. There is ointment everywhere. The left side of my face looks mostly like it did yesterday, only it, too, is swollen. Comparing the two sides is like night and day. I think of Two-Face from Batman. Despite largely expecting to see what I'm seeing, it is shocking—one of those out-of-body experiences people talk about, like I'm watching myself from outside of myself. I wonder if my parents are thinking the same thing that crosses my mind.

How will I ever be beautiful now? Despite the stinging, the tears flow down, down, down as I wonder whether the salt in them could be good for my wound.

We sit in silence for a few minutes until there is a knock at the door, and, without waiting for a response, Alessandro and Vittoria come in with my pizza. Aside from feeling the need to wipe my tears away, their timing couldn't be better. Instead of reinforcing the waves of nausea, the smell not only overrides it, but I suddenly feel like I could eat a whole cow. I realize I have no idea how long it's been since I've eaten a meal.

"Serah, I told you not to get in a fight with a rabid vampire! They *always* win," Alessandro offers. He wraps his arm around me, taps my back in a gentle hug, and makes himself comfortable at the foot of my bed. I force a laugh while my dad smiles at Alessandro, and my mom gives him a death stare for the joke. Vittoria is much slower to approach, like she's found a wounded bobcat in the bush and wants to help but senses danger.

"H—how are you, baby sister?" Vittoria gets out.

"I've been better. I don't think all the makeup you own can help me now. But maybe the pizza will, just a little." They all LOL, which seems like an overreaction. Alessandro hands over the box, and when I open the lid, I find two pieces missing already.

"That was me," Alessandro confesses. "I couldn't help it. I had to track down Mike, the owner, and convince him that he should cook you a pizza before heading to Laytonsville for the evening. All he had time for was one. He's probably going to be stuck in traffic, but when I told him you looked like Frankenstein, and it was my fault, he caved."

I grin to let him know I appreciate it—but secretly want to stab him for eating some.

"Thank you," is what comes out. He must feel really bad.

"I'm so sorry, Serah-boo." And now it's his turn. He came in with his typical seventeen-year-old macho act, but it didn't take long for his shell to crack. Alessandro bursts into uncontrollable tears. I've never seen him cry, except maybe as a ten-year-old who got hit by a baseball. Vittoria is still taking it all in.

"The accident wasn't your fault, Alessandro." My dad tries to console him, but he is sobbing. My seemingly invincible brother is heaving and shaking. I decide the way to make him feel better is to try to eat while the pizza is still warm.

"Alessandro, look, my mouth still works!" It hurts to move my arm toward my mouth, but I raise the pizza to my face, gingerly take a bite, and am amazed at how food could ever taste so good. It even seems to soothe my sore throat. I "ooh" and "ahh" to let him know that his errand to track down Pizza Brama for me was above and beyond.

He smiles a little and calms down.

"I should have known nothing could stop your brain and, thus, your mouth. I'm so sorry we never made it there last night, Serah-boo."

"We never made it where?"

At this, Vittoria perks up a little and gives my mom a worried glance. Alessandro does as well, like they all know something I don't know. My mom silences them with her hands and face, trying to reassure them and indicating that Alessandro can respond.

"I had just gotten you from soccer last night, and we were heading to pick up Pizza Brama when—"

"When the accident happened," my dad finishes.

"I don't remember that. But maybe that's why it was on my mind as soon as I woke up." I struggle to feed myself and get a little frustrated. "Can someone cut it up into bites and feed me?" I ask. "I'm starving, and for the first time in my life, I can't stuff my own face."

"I'll do it," Alessandro says, and my mom smiles.

"When you've had enough, I think it would be a good idea for you to try to rest some more. Your father and I will be staying at the hospital until you're released, and Nonna is already at the house so that she can stay with your brother and sister through the weekend."

"Will she come and see me?" I ask.

"*Ovviamente, caro mio.* Now, get some rest."

Luckily, after finishing the pizza rather quickly, I feel full and ready to sleep again somehow. And in no time, with my entire family watching over me, I'm out like a light.

Chapter 14:
BETRAYAL

"Mercy"
—SHAWN MENDES

Everything has beauty, but not everyone sees it.
—CONFUCIUS

When I wake up and open my one good eye, I see that my nonna and mom are both in the room, chatting quietly in Italian. My mom's mom is the epitome of the family woman, a matriarch with the most. Her name is Amalia, which means "hardworking." And boy, is she ever. She wears all of her seven decades of life on her face.

There is a small slit between my right eyelids now, so I can just make out some light coming in, but that's it. Turning my head toward the window—the source of the light—stops their conversation, and they both look at me, expectantly.

"*Mio Tesoro*!" my grandmother gushes. She is swift for her seventy-something years, reaching my bed in seconds. "How-uh you-ah feeling?" she intones with her thick accent.

"I've been better. How do I look?"

"*Eri meglio primo*," Nonna says.

"*Mammina*!" my mom hisses at her. I guess it's good I don't speak Italian.

"Fine-uh. You look-uh like-ah branzino who lost his fight-uh with a fisherman."

"Very funny, Nonna."

"You go home tomorrow or Monday. You be fine-eh."

"Which means it's Saturday already. I must be missing my soccer game."

"There will be plenty of time to play soccer when you haven't been through a traumatic car accident," my mom says in her mom voice. I raise my good eyebrow at her.

"So the accident was traumatic?"

My mom ignores me, and I realize I *still* have so many questions.

"What happened to the other driver? Is he okay?"

"*She* is fine. She was wearing her seatbelt and has minor scrapes and bruises but walked away, just like Alessandro. It's like your father said; it could have been so much worse."

"How did it happen?"

"The other driver was texting and didn't look up to see that her light had changed from green to red. She went right through it and slammed into you guys."

I think about this. I've heard of texting causing accidents, but it's one thing to know it happens and another to experience it. I realize my face doesn't hurt as much when I talk today, and I have a little more energy. My body, though, still feels very sore, and my arms and legs feel heavy.

"What time is my soccer game today?"

"The good news is you seem to be very alert and have good recall. The bad news is you're driving me crazy with all your questions."

"You should rest, *il mio amore*," my nonna chimes in.

"But if my brain is working properly, and that clock is right, I believe I have now slept almost a day and a half straight. What I need is food. And maybe to go to my soccer game to be there for my team."

"Number one, your game is at eleven. Two, we can order you whatever you'd like to eat. And three, there's no way you're leaving here before tomorrow. But if you'd like, I can see if the team can come here to see you after the game."

"Of course! Ohmigosh, yes, please text all the moms! And as for food, how about pancakes, French toast, scrambled eggs, bacon, sausage links, and orange juice?"

"On the way. I'll run down to the cafeteria to get it because that will be fastest. Nonna can stay with you." My mom heads for the door, giving us a wink before she leaves.

"Your parents . . . so-uh scare when they call me, amore."

"I can imagine."

"No. No, you don't. They-uh love you so, so much."

"I know."

My grandmother gazes at my face, taking me in like only grandparents can. I wonder if she's worried about my wounds. I wonder what she sees now when she looks at me. It's like she can read my mind.

"Even witt dis-uh (she points at my messed-up face), you a very beautiful girl, Seraphina."

"Thanks, Nonna. You're beautiful too."

"Me? Nooooooooooo." She shakes her head in disbelief.

Out of sympathy alone, I realize my grandmother is going to do whatever I ask, including answer my questions.

"What makes you say that?"

"Well, I jus-ah am old. In English, I 'no spring-uh chicken.'"

"But you don't have to be young to be beautiful. Or, as I'm learning, super attractive."

"Seraphina, I tink-uh your accident has-ah change your brain."

Is this my concussion? Or have I gone to crazy town? My grandmother is looking at the mess I am in this hospital bed and calling it beautiful. She sees past all the stitches and bruises and sees *me* and whatever beauty I have. But herself?

"Nonna, it's not the accident. You ARE beautiful."

"Why you say?" She doesn't believe me.

"You care for us, cook for us, serve us. You worked hard all your life to provide for your family and love your children. You risked everything, left all that was familiar, to come here and give your family a good life. You're here to help us now. You're gentle and kind. And I think your eyes, like mine, are really beautiful."

If another family member cries in front of me, I don't think I'll be able to handle it. At least, unlike my dad and brother, I've seen my Nonna cry.

"You so sweet, Seraphina. My little angel," she says as she gently rubs my good cheek with the back of her hand.

"A fiery-winged one," I add.

"Yes, yes. You always been-uh . . . *coraggioso y ardente*."

"I probably get it from you."

"Maybe," she shrugs. "You rest. I sit with you."

I close my good left eye and do as she says. Just knowing she's here and imagining my team coming to see me make me happy. I'm not sure how much time goes by with her watching me lie here, but my mom returns seemingly quickly with two bags of food, plastic utensils, and a tray to hold it all on my hospital bed.

"*Mangia*," my mom says. She always uses more Italian when Nonna's around. "Some of your teammates will try to visit after the game. It won't be too many so you don't get overwhelmed. Mrs. Caldwell would also like to visit."

"Mrs. Caldwell? But—"

"Word travels fast, and because she's your guidance counselor, she was concerned. Plus, your dad and I thought perhaps seeing her would be helpful."

"Why's that?" I ask, but I think I know.

"Mrs. Caldwell knows what it's like to be where you are. When your dad treated her years ago, she was in a very fragile state. We've always kept in touch."

When my dad WHAT?

"Wait—huh?"

"What?" my mom says, looking confused.

"Did you just say dad treated Mrs. Caldwell?"

"Oh, yes, I did. I thought you knew that." Her momentary relief that I wasn't confused by what she had said—as she searches for any sign of brain damage—is quickly set aside with new concern that this is information I didn't already have.

I can't believe what a bombshell she has dropped. My brain quickly dismisses the idea that perhaps there's another Mrs. Caldwell my mom could be talking about. My parents . . . know . . . Nadia Caldwell? My dad treated her? How is this the first time I've ever heard this? How could I be assigned to her at school if she has a relationship with my parents? I've been blindsided for the second time in two days; only, this one might hurt more.

And now I panic. *What* has she told them? What have *they* told *her*?

"Let me get this straight. Daddy treated Mrs. Caldwell as a patient? For what, her face?"

"Yes, sweetie, years ago, when she had her own . . . accident."

"Are you friends with her?"

"Nooooo, we're not . . . *friends*. We're friend*ly*. She's been through a lot, so we've kept in touch over the years here and there."

"Do you talk about . . . me?" I manage to choke out, wondering if my mom would tell me the truth if they did.

"No, sweetheart, we haven't spoken in ages. She called me as soon as she heard, worried about you."

I look away. I'm not sure if I believe her. *How long is ages*? I want to ask, but I drop it because no matter what her next answer is, it won't make me feel better.

I feel so betrayed. I'm wondering what, if anything, from the past few months Mrs. Caldwell has told my parents about me and our talks. Now it makes sense that Mrs. Caldwell suggested I speak with my mom. And how the last time we talked, it felt like there was something she was going to say but didn't. And how the entire room changed when she mentioned my mom. What a joke! How *dare* she!

"I do not want to see her. Please don't have her come here," is all I can manage to get out.

"Okay, Serah, it's okay. You don't have to. I don't see what the big deal is, but of course, you don't have to see anyone you don't want to see right now. All you need to do is whatever will make you get better."

"I think I need to be alone while I eat," I say quietly. "Maybe some more rest is a good idea after all."

My mom frowns but tries to hide it. Nonna's not so easily swayed.

"I sit here, no make-ah no sound," she says, folding her arms over her chest as if to say, *the decision is made*.

"Fine, Nonna, you can stay."

◦ ✳ ◦

After eating in silence with my grandmother watching me—a very uncomfortable way to eat—I decide to watch some TV. When you're watching live television on Saturday morning in spring, your options are apparently golf, little kid cartoons, and infomercials. Luckily, my parents brought my iPod and charger, and for the first time in two days, I look at it.

I have a bajillion messages. People I didn't even know I knew must have gotten my email address from other people and reached out to send me "get well soon," "feel better," "glad ur ok!" texts and even attempts at funny messages, like "I can't try to cheat off u now!"

Courtney, of course, has sent me two hundred texts to tell me she loves me, hopes I'm okay, tried to sneak out of her house and get to me, tried to break into the hospital during non-visiting hours, and got caught for everything. She says it's okay I'm not answering any of her questions but that she'll try to come and visit after our game. She's also apologized about getting involved in the Liv and Jessica drama, saying she believes me and never should have doubted me.

The Liv and Jessica drama! I had completely forgotten about the whole PE swim disaster.

Jessica and Liv have both sent me about fifty texts each to say they're sorry; they don't care about what happened in the pool; they hope I can forgive them, and they've talked about how dumb their fight was. That's good news, I guess.

I mean, there's nothing like a real accident—not a "fake kicking"—to bring people together and point out how stupid imaginary problems and sixth-grade girl drama are. I still want to talk to Liv about things, so I decide to write her back right away.

> Liv, I just got my iPod. I'm ok. Thx for ur texts

> I just want to know if u made up the kick part of the story, or if Jessica actually kicked u

> It's SO GOOD to know ur Ok!!! TBH, Jess lightly bumped me, but I made a big deal of it. I know she didn't kick me on purpose

> Ok. Then why would u say she did?

> I guess I was jealous. It's hard to share u in PE. I'm really sorry

> It's ok. I forgive you.
> Tho FWIW, Jess is pretty cool.
> Did u tell Court the truth?

No, but I will after our game.
Can I come c u?

> Of course!

I'm really glad all that seems to be over. I'm also grateful that Courtney has my back, and even without Liv telling her the truth, she believes me.

But maybe the most welcome texts I've gotten are from the same number that sent me the poop messages. I realize I'm holding my breath as I click on the chain.

Serah, I heard u got in a
car accident. U ok?

Sorry I wrote those other texts.
It was dumb. I hope u r alright

(8 hours later)

Lemme know ur ok

I decide to write back. After all, it could be Nick or Carter, or even a girl. I keep holding my breath as I text:

144

Christine Virgin

> Who is this?

(The ... bubble appears.)

> Seth

EEK! It's really him, which makes me a little sad to know *for sure* for sure that he sent those messages. But I also don't know what to say. How can I write him back without sounding like I'm into him?

> I'm in the hospital, but ok

> My g-ma says I've looked better.
> At least I think that's what
> she said in Italian

> Ha! u could never look that bad

I feel a little flutter in my stomach.

> Thx

I don't want to write too many words and sound like I care too much.

> I have 2 go but I'm glad ur ok.
> Cya at school, I hope

> you too

145

I type that but think maybe it sounds like I'm desperate. So I erase it.

> K. Bye!

Better. I think I handled that pretty well. And I begin to think that maybe Seth's not so bad. Maybe I should forgive him. Besides, I have someone new to be mad at anyway.

I flip through more messages while chewing on some bacon, trying to distract myself from thinking about Mrs. Caldwell or wishing Seth would show up with flowers. Then I'm grateful he hasn't, and probably won't, because I know I still look awful.

I lick the bacon grease off my fingers and wipe them on my napkin so I can write back to Courtney.

> All is well. I'm ok. Win the game 4 me and then come see me. K?

> Done and done. SOOO good to hear your voice. U know what I mean. Will I be scared when I see u?

> Alessandro called me Frankenstein. So prolly. u'll have to see 4 yourself.

> No more info until you
> score and come see me!!!!

I put down the phone and stuff a few more bites of mediocre French toast into my mouth as my mind returns to Mrs. Caldwell. The food and texts were a welcome distraction, but now my head is spinning from reading, and I'm nauseated, probably a combination of my mom's news, my injuries, whatever drugs they're giving me, and stuffing my empty stomach with hospital food. I decide to close my good eye so I can rest until my teammates arrive.

◎ ❀ ◎

I wish I could say it was good to see Courtney, Liv, Katie, and other teammates like Diana, Priya, and Zabrina. But their reaction to my face is just like my family's— some trying to make me laugh, others not even knowing what to say but looking afraid. They're trying hard to make me feel better with a play-by-play description of the game. But laughing still hurts a lot, and knowing they won just makes it suck that I wasn't there to be a part of it. Stink, not suck. And now my mind is back on Mrs. Caldwell *again*, only this time remembering her correcting me for using that language. She's the one who sucks. I mean stinks. UGH.

"So when can you go home? We should have a party to celebrate!" Courtney gushes.

"Probably tomorrow," I say as I look at my mom hopefully, and she puts her hands in the air as if to say, "We'll see."

"Will you be at school on Monday?" Katie asks.

"We still have to figure out her longer-term recovery in regard to school and getting back to normal life," my mom answers for me.

I hadn't thought of that until now. There are only a couple of weeks until school gets out for summer. I would love to go back and finish the year, but the thought of showing up looking like this is more than I can imagine right now. I could stay home and avoid having to see most people altogether until the fall.

"I don't think I'll feel ready to be back on Monday but maybe later in the week," I think out loud.

"It won't be the same without you," Courtney says with a frown.

"I know," I say, winking my left eye, which makes everyone laugh. "I'm so glad you came."

At this, Katie's mom mentions needing to get everyone home so they can get on with their Saturdays, and I suddenly feel lonely even though everyone is still here. But a small part of me is grateful they're leaving so I can go back to sleep. And when I do, I am restless, dreaming of my parents hanging out with Mrs. Caldwell and her husband, laughing and talking about me.

Chapter 15:
BEAUTY DEFINED

"Broken and Beautiful".
—KELLY CLARKSON

A woman becomes beautiful
when she knows she's loved.
—STASI ELDREDGE, *CAPTIVATING*

My parents were right. And, like every kid, I hate to admit it. I was released on Sunday, but my recovery was far from over. I had to stay home from school for the entire week.

It's now Friday again, one week since my accident. And I'm bored out of my mind. I'm staring out the family room window, trying to get some take-home schoolwork done but struggling to focus. I'm so distracted by everything: wondering what's happening at school without me, wondering what people are saying, wondering how awful people are saying I look, or if they're talking about me at all. I'm not sure which would be worse, but I think people not talking at all would be worse than them saying mean things. I remember last year when Sally had to miss more than a week of school to get her tonsils taken out. People seemed genuinely concerned. As I'm somewhat comforted by that thought, the doorbell rings. My mom, ever-the-nurse, tells me not to move. She jogs to the front door, which I can't see from the family room. But it's just around a wall so that I can hear.

"Oh, hi, Nadia! I'm so glad you are here! Please, come in," I hear my mom say.

"I'm sorry to drop in like this, but you did say anytime would be good, and this was a break in my schedule at school."

I would recognize that annoyingly perfect, sweet, and kind voice anywhere. It's Mrs. Caldwell. At my house. She has the nerve to show up *at my house*! I feel both anger and panic rise so quickly that I don't know what to do, paralyzing me. Besides, I still can't move all that quickly yet anyway, so there's no bounding up the stairs secretly before they round the corner. There is nowhere to hide—nowhere I can run and escape what's about to happen, which is infuriating. For a second, I consider pretending that I've lost my sight and hearing from the accident. I see Mrs. Caldwell pop her bubbly head around the wall with a wary, arched eyebrow smile. Then she extends her arm around the corner, which holds a bouquet of flowers. A peace offering. My mom passes around behind her, smiling that smile that indicates she decided it would be easier to ask for forgiveness than permission. I want to hurl my notebooks across the room at her head. But I don't. Not because of my mom but because I don't want to do that in front of Mrs. Caldwell.

"I see *your friend* is here, Mom," is all I can get out. Just like Liv was trying to make it clear to Jessica that Jessica was *not* her friend, I am trying to make it clear to Mrs. Caldwell that she is not mine. I did not invite her here or have anything to do with this. It sounds so mean, so not like me, but the truth is I'm trying not to cry as I feel the betrayal, anger, and confusion from the hospital rise within me all over again.

Instead of responding, my mom bows out of the room quietly, saying she knows we must have some catching up to do and wants to give us privacy. Funny—privacy with Mrs. Caldwell is the last thing I want.

"Oh, Serah, I've thought so much about you since I heard about your accident. Would it be okay to sit down?"

As much as I want to go off on her, my only response is a half-hearted shrug.

"It is really amazing how much you have healed already. You look really, really great."

I offer nothing.

"Serah, your mom told me you are angry with me. With us."

You could say that again.

"I'm not sure what she has told you, but I want you to know that I never meant to hurt you, and everything I've done, I've done with the best intentions."

Don't most people not mean to hurt you? I mean, sometimes, people are intentionally mean, like Veruca and Cecilia, but often when we hurt people, it's by accident.

"Serah, I didn't share with you that I knew your parents because I didn't want that to keep you from opening up to me. I was waiting for the right time to tell you. Looking back now, I can see that was the wrong decision. The school assigned you to me six years ago, and I went to Mr. Rooney and told him about my acquaintance with your parents. Once he knew all the details, he determined there was no conflict of interest to me being your counselor."

I still have nothing to say, though it is slightly comforting to know that they at least considered me.

"You were five years old at the time. We decided it better to keep it quiet so you could open up to me and build our rapport. And as you've gotten older, I've been looking for the right time to tell you. In fact, every time you've come to me this year, I've wanted to say something. But I chickened out. I was afraid that you'd want to change counselors, and then you'd have to build trust with someone new, which can take time. Plus, Serah, I really, truly care for you and didn't want you to go through that simply because I knew your parents from years ago."

I'm still quiet.

"As all of what we talk about is privileged information, I decided, somewhat selfishly, that I would wait to tell you at the end of the school year. I knew it would be impossible to tell you that I had a relationship with your parents without explaining the 'how' to you, and there's no way to explain the *how* without sharing some deeply private, personal information. Unfortunately, you found out before I could tell you."

I consider everything she is saying to me without looking at her. I take some deep, calming breaths. I stop my silent treatment.

"What does privileged mean here?"

"In this case, privileged information means I can't share it with anyone. Unless I were afraid you were a threat to yourself or someone else, I couldn't tell anyone what we talked about in our meetings."

I shift in my seat. Part of me wants to keep holding up the heavy wall I built between us over the past week, but the weight of it is starting to crush me. And if what she is saying is true, she hasn't talked to my mom, or anyone, about *anything*.

"Not even my parents?"

"Nope. They know you can come talk to me at school, but they don't know when you've done that. They don't know what we've talked about. I have not shared any details."

I let out a long sigh, still staring off into space.

"Serah, I'm so sorry. Your dad was one of my doctors years ago when I went through an extraordinarily difficult time." The wall comes tumbling down enough to allow me to look her in the eyes. I realize that I'm about to get answers to some of the questions I never had the guts to ask. "Alessandro was a kindergartener at the school, and I had met your parents at back-to-school night weeks before my . . . incident. When I arrived at the hospital, your father was the plastic surgeon on call. He recognized me. After my surgeries, your mom and dad helped coordinate some care for me and checked in on me."

I think about what she is saying and roll it around in my mind. I still want to be mad, but I'm so relieved to be getting answers. And I realize that I can probably get her to tell me anything I want to know now. This is my chance because she owes me *big time*.

"Why was my dad your plastic surgeon? For the scar on your face?"

"Yes." She doesn't offer details.

"Mrs. Caldwell, what happened? Were you in a car accident too?"

I hear her take a deep breath through her nostrils and blow the air out of her mouth.

"No, Serah, I wasn't in a car accident. I was attacked."

"Attacked?! When? Why? How?"

She smiles. "I told you there was no way to tell you about my relationship with your parents without explaining the backstory." She looks down, the first signal she's ever given me of discomfort. "I was attacked by a man whom I barely knew."

She pauses. "He wanted something from me that I wouldn't give him, and he didn't like that, so he pulled out a knife."

I'm on the edge of my seat, leaning in, rubbing the sweat that's developing on my palms onto my lap. "And then what?"

"Well, although it was dark out, I was in a public place, and my hope was someone, anyone, would pass by. I tried to reason with him to buy some time, but he was holding me, and I couldn't get away."

She looks at me, and I urge her to continue with my silence.

"Then we both heard two voices coming our way, people walking while having a conversation. It gave me hope! But I think it made him mad. I'll never forget what he did next. He put his mouth to my ear and whispered, 'I'm going to make sure you remember me for the rest of your life.' Then he attacked me with the knife, and I passed out. I have no memory of anything between that moment and waking up in the hospital from surgery more than twenty-four hours later."

O. M. Gosh.

"Was he trying to rob you? Why didn't you just give him what he wanted? Then you probably wouldn't have been attacked with the knife!"

"That's a really good question, Serah. I will never know, will I? And I've come to terms with that. And if I could go back in time and do it all over again, I would react the same way. I have done a lot of work to get through the trials I've faced, and I've come through all of them a better person. Everything I've experienced has taught me something and helped me help others, and I know that

God continues to use my trauma for good. I have seen it time and again and have faith it will continue to happen." She waits, but I have no interest in filling the space with my words. "So much time has passed, I often forget how much my visible scar can cause curiosity. For me, it is all in the past, and frankly, I find you to be much more interesting. I'd much rather talk about how you're doing."

"But I need to know things, Mrs. Caldwell."

"What do you need to know?" she says with a sly smile. I think about my next words carefully. What I want to know and what I need to know are two different things.

"Your scar . . . what has it done to you? So I can, you know, prepare myself," I choke out, motioning toward my own cheek. I can't keep the tears that have welled in my eyes from dripping down.

"Oh gosh, Serah. At first, the scar on my face was a source of shame. It called me names in my head. It told me that what that man did was my fault. But I learned over time how to shut down that voice." She gets up to grab the tissue box that's across the room. After handing it to me and patting me on the back, she sits back down right next to me.

"My scar not only belittled me at first but also asked me questions. What did I do to deserve this? Could I have changed things? Will I ever be lovable? Will I be pretty again? But as my physical wounds healed, I uncovered that most of my scars were internal. I learned so much about myself and about how much God loves me. He helped me change a lot of things for the better. And now I get to help people."

"I guess that's good." I am not sure I'll ever think of my scar as good. But I realize that when I look at Mrs. Caldwell, I just see her. I notice the scar if I look for it, but not if I don't. Through continued tears, I know this is it. Like in the car with my mom just weeks ago, I find the strength to ask the scariest question of all.

"Mrs. Caldwell, what was the answer to your question about being pretty again?"

"Oh, that's a great question. While it took some time to get to where I am today, I am being 100 percent honest when I say I believe I am more beautiful now than I was before I had this scar."

Whahh? Did I just hear what I think I heard?

"I think you're going to have to explain that one," I admit.

She takes another deep breath, in through the nose, out through the mouth. "Serah, when I was in middle school, high school, and college, I was like Cecilia."

Cecilia who? *Who is she talking ab—oh, CECILIA.* This is an epic revelation.

"You know, Vittoria's friend you've told me about."

"Yeah, savage Cecilia. I just can't believe it. What do you mean you were 'like Cecilia'?"

"Well, I was insecure, and my parents weren't really involved in my life. They were too busy working multiple jobs to give me a good life here in the States. I looked for validation around me at school and with boys. Having emigrated from Russia, I believed my good looks were my ticket to catching a popular guy and, eventually, a guy who could provide for me. I became a jerk. I was obsessed with what people thought about me, and I basically threw myself at men for attention without caring about whose feelings I might hurt in the process. I was very attractive to them and spent a lot of time making myself look desirable."

"I'm confused. Because you were from Russia, you became a flirt?"

"Ha, noooooooo." She pauses. "It's not that simple. I think my parents taught me that the way I looked was a blessing for our family and that I could use it to find a wealthy man who could take care of me—and even them. When you aren't sure you will have food to eat, survival can dictate all your other behavior."

"That sounds really hard. My parents tell us all the time we shouldn't complain about our food because we are fortunate enough to have all we could want and more. But no matter how many times they say that, it just doesn't make Brussels sprouts edible."

She smiles warmly at me. "If it makes you feel any better, I would have gone hungry before I would have eaten Brussels sprouts at your age too." She pauses again, and we let the silence ring out for a minute.

"I'm not proud to share this with you, nor of who I used to be. After I was attacked in my twenties, I had to heal physically, mentally, and emotionally. My physical scars healed a lot more quickly than the others. I went to see a licensed therapist through my church. And that's when I really started to understand who I was in God's eyes and what my value and worth were no matter what I looked like or what status I had—no matter if I had a scar on my face or not."

I knew Mrs. Caldwell would have answers.

"And who is that?"

"Well, through my faith, I believe God created me with certain gifts, likes, and dislikes, and I'm unlike anyone else who has ever walked the planet. I believe he loved me when I was being formed, he loved me when I was shallow, he loved me when I was attacked, he loves me now, and he will forever because there's nothing I could do to lose his love.

"Once I was secure in that—really deep down in my heart—what others thought of me started to matter less. As more and more time went on, and I worked on loving myself, my scar became less and less noticeable to me. Now when I look in the mirror, I just see me. I don't see my moles right here," she says as she points to two moles on her face, "nor the scar that's probably pretty obvious to most people."

Huh. I hesitate before saying anything.

"Well, I guess most of that makes sense. I've done a lot of research over the past few months. I'm learning about beauty and how we're all beautiful, especially girls."

Mrs. Caldwell flashes that smile again.

"Yes! A thousand times, yes. There is beauty all around us if we just look for it. The Bible says that the WHOLE earth is filled with the glory—or the weight, honor, and splendor—of God. Including people who I believe he made in his image. Everyone reflects beauty because God is beauty."

"So Cecilia?"

"You ask some tough questions," she grins. "But yes, even Cecilia is beautiful. My guess is she doesn't know it."

"Mrs. Caldwell?"

"Yes, Serah?"

"I'm scared."

"Of what?"

"Of my scar. Of how people will see me differently. Of being called names. Of believing it makes me ugly. Of how people will point or giggle or say mean things behind my back, or . . . everything!"

"Serah, this experience is going to teach you so much and make you stronger. My advice is to take things one day at a time. Your courage will build every time you face one of those fears and prove it wrong."

"Mrs. Caldwell?"

She nods.

"I'm sorry I was mad. I thought all sorts of things that weren't true. I'm glad my parents were able to help you years ago before I was born."

"Yeah, your mom was pregnant with you AND working and taking care of Vittoria and Alessandro, and she brought me food once a week for several months just to check in on me."

Whoa.

"That was . . . really nice of her."

"It was. There were so many people who supported me, just like they will support you. You will get through this. It will change you, but for the better."

"Thanks for coming over."

"You're welcome. But I should probably let you rest or get to your schoolwork now. Although out of all students, missing a couple weeks of school probably won't affect you at all. You are intelligent AND beautiful. What a special combination."

I blush. And now I wonder again about just what Mrs. Caldwell and my mom have talked about. Although Mrs. Caldwell's conversations with me are "privileged," my mom's are not. But as I look at my counselor and think about my mom, I decide to believe that she came up with that on her own.

"I'm supposed to be back at the office already," she laments.

"Then get back to work!" I say, saluting like I'm a drill sergeant. It feels good to have a sliver of fun in all the seriousness of the moment.

"It was worth it to stay. Even if I get detention," she ponders playfully.

"Wait, do they actually give detention to *teachers*?!"

Giggling, she responds, "Ah, Serah, for someone so wise and smart, you are incredibly gullible."

I smile. I slowly rise to walk her to the door, which she lets me do.

"Oh, wait, do you want to say anything to my mom?"

"No, I'm fine. Please tell her I appreciate her letting me drop in and give her my best."

"Gotcha."

And as I close the door, I race upstairs, surprised by my ability to move so quickly.

I pull out the Beautiful List from my desk, take one last look at it, and know what to do.

Chapter 16:
SUMMER

"Girl in the Mirror"
—BEBE REXHA

*God's love looks for those who feel unlovely, desiring
to make them beautiful again.*
—NATALIE GRANT

It's Sunday, the day before I will go back to school for the first time since the accident. Being home for two weeks has given me a lot of space to heal and think. It has also caused a lot of fights with my parents because I felt ready to go back to school as soon as I got home from the hospital. (Okay, maybe not then but a few days later.) To spite them and their overprotectiveness, I lazed around and binge-watched every season of *Best Friends Whenever* and secretly got through several episodes of *Parks and Recreation* before getting caught. When my mom complained, I reminded

163

her that the doctor's orders were to rest, and I would happily get dressed and go to school. That shut her up. 😑

While home, I've gotten all sorts of texts from people, too, which has been nice 'cause I've kept up with what's going on. Friends, teammates, and even somewhat random people from school have bugged me for the whole story. I've gotten so many questions, from how badly it hurt (um, probably like getting mauled by a liger), to how hard I bled (my clothes were so gross I had to throw them out), to whether the EMTs were hot (that was Liv, and I have no idea 'cause I was unconscious), to wondering if I cried (again, I was unconscious). And the most requested thing of all: a selfie of what I looked like. Mandy King even had the nerve to ask for one. #asif

I did not take a picture in the hospital. I didn't want to. I also didn't want to take one until I thought I looked more like a person and less like a zombie apocalypse survivor. After Mrs. Caldwell left my house, I decided I wanted to document the healing of my scar, sort of like a before and after and along-the-way journal of photos. I could always delete them, I reasoned, but never go back and take pictures I hadn't taken.

Of course, I didn't send the pictures to anyone except Courtney. I knew she wouldn't share them. Aside from bugging me about my choice of TV shows, my mom was super nice to me the whole time I was stuck at home. She took me shopping on Tuesday and let me pick out everything I tried on, which was probably a challenge for her, seeing as she still wants me to wear poodle skirts. She even let me have friends over on weeknights this week to help me with some schoolwork. Jessica was a lifesaver! But I can't even describe with words how nervous excited I am to go back to school, even if it's only for one week before summer break.

This morning, I'm wearing my favorite outfit and my bravest face, and I'm walking up the sidewalk to the main doors with shaky confidence. Before opening them, I take a deep breath to prepare myself for what's to come. I can see my reflection in the thin, glass rectangle above the door handle, with its crisscross wire pattern between the panes. My scar stares back at me. Even in the glass, I can see it. I change focus to the rest of my face, open the door, and will my legs to walk.

As I pass the first set of classrooms full of lower schoolers, it's like any other school day and almost feels like no time has passed at all. The younger kids barely notice me. But as I get to the end of the hall, closer to fourth and fifth grades, where I have to turn the corner to get to the sixth-grade classrooms, people begin recognizing me, mostly in a good way, to give me high fives or hugs. One fourth-grade girl named Samantha, who broke her arm sometime in the past two weeks, asks me to sign her cast immediately.

I settle into my usual seat in homeroom, and, of course, Veruca comes over and does all the right things to act like she cares, but I know she is just trying to get a good look at me up close. My scar is pretty bright red, and I have to keep ointment on it all the time, as well as wear a hat ALL summer to keep the sun off of it. My neck scar is pretty noticeable, too, but smaller. I hear her talking but am not paying attention, just watching her examine me like I'm bacteria under a microscope. And I realize that maybe my parents wanted me to skip a second week of school not for my body to heal but for my face to look better. It's been seventeen days, and my face is still bruised. Parts of my body are still a little sore.

Our first-period teacher, Mr. Crouch, asks everyone to stop crowding me and get to their seats so we can get started with our day. And then he welcomes me back, saying he is grateful I am okay and that the class has not been the same without me. I can feel my face flush and then imagine that my scar must be less noticeable when I'm embarrassed.

Our yearbooks have arrived, so Mr. Crouch spends our time in home period passing them out. He gives us the rest of the period to sign them because he knows asking us *not* to would be like asking our cat to lie on her back in our pool and float peacefully. I notice the girls have started writing longer notes this year. I thought maybe it was just me because of my accident, but as I sign other yearbooks, I notice lots of full-on letters filling the pages. My yearbook might have the funniest messages EVER in it. Courtney wrote:

"It's impossible to know how important someone is to you until their absence from the same building—even if you hardly ever see them there—is something that HURTS. I'm so glad you made it back, gimp! Try not to eat any more windshields, and I can't wait to kick some serious soccer butt with you next year!! To the BEST BFF EVER!!!! ♥ COURT."

A few other people make jokes about my accident, like Jessica and Liv, who get along "swimmingly" in PE the whole last week of school, to my pleasure. I'm not allowed to swim yet, so I spend PE every day catching up on some schoolwork and wishing I could be in the water. It's funny how you want what you can't have because I should be grateful I don't have to change into a bathing suit and show my nipples to everyone. I did actually send a letter to Speedo while I was recovering. We'll see what happens.

Most of the boys write very little in yearbooks. Just their names and maybe two or three words is normal, or maybe if they're artsy, they have started drawing video game characters or cars they're into. I had decided while I was stuck at home that I wasn't going to ask Seth Rodriguez to sign my yearbook, but that if *he* wanted to, I would act cool like it was no big deal. I notice him heading toward me with his book while I'm signing Sonya's, and I can feel my heart start beating louder and faster.

"Hey, Serah, will you sign my yearbook?"

Sensing my tomato-face, I keep my head down and mutter, "Sure," like I don't care at all. He sets his yearbook down on my desk but doesn't walk away.

"Can I sign yours?"

My heart skips a beat as I try to act bored.

"Sure," I say again, mortified by my inability to string two intelligent words together when I speak to him. I make eye contact for the shortest moment and realize my crush is not gone. It's possible I ended my yearbook note to Sonya with "Ohmigosh ohmigosh ohmigosh."

When he hands the book back, I read:

"Serah, stay cool, keep healing, and have a great break. Glad you're OK! Keep in touch," with his phone number there. At first, I think he is an idiot if he can't remember that I already have his number, but then I feel my face get red again as I think maybe he wrote it down just to be sure I would never lose it. I also realize it's not a bad note, but it's also not swoon-worthy. I was hoping for, "Serah, this is the perfect chance to declare my massive crush on you. I only texted you dumb things because I'm a dumb boy who doesn't know how to say I like you. Please put me out of my misery and text me this summer so we can hang out!!! XOXO, Seth." But I guess "stay cool" with his number is better than just "have a good summer." That's what you write in people's yearbooks when you don't have anything to say to them. Plus, I might have sabotaged my chances anyway with what I wrote in his yearbook. For him and Nick, I signed:

"I'm not sure why you want poop in your yearbook, but here you go. 😄 —Serah," and I drew little poops. What can I say? I can't help it.

Now we're even.

The summer is flying by. It's already mid-August. I have had to stay out of the sun, which has definitely sucked, er, stunk. I'm more thankful than ever for my indoor pool. My scar has already faded some. My dad even says he couldn't have done a better job.

My parents surprised me with a cell phone just this week. I'm stoked not to be entering middle school as the only kid without a real phone. They told me the same rules as my iPod apply: They can read my texts, view my browser history, and manage my apps. And if they find social media installed on it, it's gone. I'm kinda both annoyed and grateful. On the one hand, I'm going to miss out. On the other, I can't imagine opening myself up to public ridicule or popularity contests online, especially because of my scars.

It feels like they are becoming a part of me. I notice them less and less and probably wouldn't think about them that much if I didn't have to slather them with sunscreen every day. If they get me down, or I feel ugly because of them, I try to remind myself how fortunate I am to have walked away from the accident. And sometimes, I remind myself of Rachel.

I wonder what she would think of my scars. I imagine she would gush about how cool they are and help me make up really awesome stories about how I got them.

The day I met Rachel, I thought either her dad was calling her beautiful because he was trying to make her believe she was or that maybe he was trying to convince himself that she was. I didn't realize it at the time, but I now believe he was calling her beautiful *because he knew she was.* I put it right there on the Beautiful List I created only minutes later: Rachel. Right at the top. Because she had convinced me she was beautiful—because *she* embraced it.

I realize that some people will look at me and think I'm plain-looking. Some will see me and think, *She's cute*, or maybe even pretty. Some might only see my scar when they look at me. Some might even look at me and think I'm ugly. And that's okay. I know they're all wrong. Because I am beautiful.

I want to live beautiful like Rachel. Like Nadia Orlov Caldwell, one of the bravest people I know. Like my mom, who might not fully believe it about herself, but who is totally gorgeous, inside and out (and in spite of her momness). I am beginning to understand that *all* girls are beautiful; it's just that most of them don't know it.

From now on, I want to see the beauty in everything.

It turns out that beauty really is everywhere. When someone does something beautiful—an act of kindness, of giving selflessly, of using intelligence for good, of putting others first—that is true beauty.

I've come to think of my scar now as something that's just part of me, like my moles, my skin tone, my hair, and my heterochromia. All of my other accident injuries have healed, and I've been cleared to play soccer, which started a couple of weeks ago. Like so many eighth-grade relationships, Josh Swanson and Allie broke up, and he and my sister have been texting a lot. She's been showing up at my games to see him. #eyeroll #SMH

I guess I feel ready for seventh grade. I'm pretty excited that I don't have braces yet. I heard that Mandy King got them this summer, so something tells me she's going to be ultra-annoying with her comments. But I could not care less about them anymore.

And maybe the biggest newsflash of all is that my breasts have, rather suddenly, burst forth into stage two of development. And I can't wait to parade them around in all their glorious splendor in a real bra in the locker room.

Take THAT, Veruca.

Acknowledgments

First, I thank Jesus, without whom I would not grasp my beauty nor know my worth. I know this is God's project; I look forward to him using it for his purposes.

Second, to my family: Thank you, Greg, for encouraging me to "go big" on that date night when I told you I was working on this. You and the kids have had my back. As I write this acknowledgment, I know you will continue to sacrifice as I push this out to the world.

To my parents, Larry and Brigitte Elliott: Mom, thanks for being one of my first readers and for your unfailing love and support. Dad, thanks for believing I could do it and for editing my papers as I was growing up.

To Mr. Ray Anastas, Mrs. Dana Mullaney, Mrs. Jean Newman, Ms. Susan Ashbridge, Dr. Charlie Tuggle, and Dr. Tom Linden: Thank you for teaching me grammar and how to write. Teachers are the world's true heroes. Last but not least on this list, Mrs. Sandy Melillo: Thanks for being my honors and AP English teacher, who introduced me to *Pride and Prejudice*. I am proof that failing the AP exam does not mean you can't become a writer. 😜

To my beta readers, Eliza Virgin, Angelika Rampal Springer, Tricia Staible, Mandy Hickerson, Rupal Mistry, Alexa Whiteside, Alex Corgan, Misie Litchiewski, Lindsey Spector, Kelly Tanzi, Enna McNeil, Gloria McNeil, Andria Crawley, and Gabriela Moore: Your feedback shaped this story and made me believe I had written something people would actually want to read.

To my college bestie and marketer extraordinaire, Melissa Sowry: How you found time to design my website and coach me through Wix is still beyond me. Thank you for stepping in when I didn't know what to do. Your yoke carried me toward publishing like nothing else did.

To Chelsea Hudson and Fleur Gedamke: You always find a way to take pictures that make me look so much better than I actually do. 🖤

To Becky Kopitzke and Katie Reed: Thank you for being my early cheerleaders. Having authors like you share your wisdom and experience with me was clutch.

To JJ Virgin, Pastor Michael White, and Lou Sabatier: Thank you for your insight and wisdom into publishing. I can't imagine having found my way through this process without you.

To Beth Lottig, my editor: After more "nos" than I want to count, you offered your time to a random aspiring author because you believed in this little project. You are the first stranger who read my manuscript. Because you believed in this story, I believed in myself. You lit the fire under me that I needed to bring this to print. Without you, I honestly might still be looking for a developmental editor. 😵

To Megan Dillon and Chris Treccani: Your design brought Serah to life and transformed her story from a manuscript into a book. Thank you for your attention to detail and creativity.

To the entire team at Morgan James Publishing responsible for pushing this into the world: I APPRECI-ATE YOU. To Cortney Donelson: thank you for picking up the phone and sharing my heart for girls. To David L. Hancock: you're one-of-a-kind. To Heidi Nickerson, Emily Madison, and Jim Howard: I'm grateful for your guidance. To Amber Parrott: get it together. And to anyone at Morgan James who touched this project, I'm indebted to you. Thank you all for taking a chance on me, coaching me, and being who you are. What's next? 😉

Author's Note

Thank you so much for reading! If you loved Serah's story, please let the world know by leaving a review online wherever you purchased the book. It might seem like a small thing, but especially for a new author, it's hugely important.

In the next pages, I've created a discussion guide for a book club. There are special add-ons and other cool products on the book's website:

WWW.THEBEAUTIFULLIST.COM

Please check it out!

Book Club
DISCUSSION GUIDE

Hi, friends and readers! This guide is here for you to dig deeper into many of the important topics covered in the book. Even reading these on your own or with a friend might help you uncover some interesting tidbits about beautiful, unique you! The guide covers two chapters a week for eight weeks but can be condensed into four weeks that cover four chapters each. If you want to do a condensed study, be sure to read through and answer all the questions on your own, but during your four meetings, only chat through the **bolded** questions from each week so you can cover two weeks at a time. Of course, these are just suggestions. Feel free to use any or none of these prompts as you sift through the thoughts and emotions this book elicits. I'm cheering you on, whether you are working through this guide on your own, with a partner, or with a group. I hope it leads you to live beautiful!

Christine

P.S. Some people are more open than others. If you're more comfortable sharing with maybe one or two other people you already know, make sure you are with her or them for this study.

WEEK 1

1. Have you ever met anyone like Rachel? Are you more like her or more like Serah? Do you have more, less, or the same amount of confidence today about who you are than you did at age seven?

2. Do you relate to Serah's thoughts of comparison? In what ways? Can you give an example of a time you have compared yourself to someone else and felt better? What about worse?

3. **Why is comparison often described as a "trap?"**

4. What is your first impression of Serah's mom? Vittoria? Alessandro?

5. What words would you use to describe yourself? Make a list if it's helpful, and share if you're willing.

6. **Serah says, "The more people say the same thing about you over and over, the more you believe it." Is there something people have said about you repeatedly that you believe about yourself because of it? If you're willing, share it and reveal how it makes you feel.**

7. What word or words do you wish people would use to describe you?

8. Have you heard a discussion like the one among Alessandro and his friends? What was said? What do you think about it?

9. Serah's favorite physical trait is her eyes. Her least favorite is her legs. Do you have a favorite and least favorite trait about yourself?

Homework: Either make your own beautiful list OR draw a color picture of Serah's face based on her description of herself. Be as detailed as possible. Keep it somewhere safe for now.

WEEK 2

1. Does anyone want to share her beautiful list or her drawing of Serah?

2. Have you ever seen a show that has emphasized the importance of outer beauty? Which one, and what did you think of it?

3. **When is it okay to have plastic surgery? Is reconstructive plastic surgery a good or a bad thing? What about cosmetic surgery?**

4. **Would it surprise you to think that everyone you know has insecurities? Why or why not?**

5. Is there anyone here who does not have any insecurities?

6. Think of someone you know who is very confident. Now think about whether you can think

of any evidence of insecurity that person has by
things you've heard them say.

7. **When friends or family criticize themselves,
   how does that affect you?**

8. What do you think about Mrs. Caldwell? Does
   your school provide counselors? Would you trust
   them enough to go to them about puberty or anything else? Why or why not?

9. **Do you have a trusted adult in your life whom
   you can talk to about anything, whether it be a
   school counselor, therapist, family member, or
   mentor? If so, who is it? If not, can you think
   of someone you can risk sharing deeper things
   with?**

10. What sorts of changes are you dealing with regard-
    ing your body? Do they scare you? Has anyone
    made fun of you for the changes you are under-
    going?

Homework: Try to think of someone you know who
has zero insecurities. If you have the chance, interview the
person to see if you are right.

WEEK 3

1. Before diving into Chapters 5 and 6, was anyone
   able to think of someone who has no insecurities?
   Did anyone ask family members, friends, or others
   about their insecurities? What did you find?

2. **Do you think Alessandro's explanation of his "hot or not" conversation explains it well enough? Excuses it? Why or why not?**

3. How would you define attraction? What about a crush?

4. **How would you define "boy crazy?" Are you or anyone you know boy crazy? Do you think it's a good or a bad thing to be boy crazy? Why or why not?**

5. Serah loves soccer; it's an outlet for her. She says, "Learning to work together toward the same goal, carrying each other's mistakes and celebrating each other's strengths, is empowering." Do you have any hobbies or outlets in your life that make you feel this way? If not, can you think of something you'd be interested in and willing to try?

6. Do the classes you have in school make you feel dumb? Smart? Neither? Both?

7. **Think of a trait one of your best friends has that you don't have and wish you did. If you're willing, share how this makes you feel.**

8. **Now, think of a gift you have that a friend of yours has noticed or pointed out to you. Does it make you feel good? Special? Guilty?**

9. Do you have an embarrassing doctor story that helps you relate to Serah's visit to the dermatologist? Share if you're able!

10. **What part of puberty are you most afraid of? What about most comfortable with?**

Homework: Write out any questions you have about puberty that you might find embarrassing. Put each on a scrap of notebook or printer paper and bring it to the next discussion group.

WEEK 4

1. Take all the puberty questions people have brought and put them in a bowl. Take fifteen minutes to draw them out one by one to answer together or with your discussion group and an adult.
2. If you have an older sister, how do you relate to Vittoria and Serah's bathroom exchange?
3. **Does your family eat dinner together rarely, sometimes, or a lot? How do your dinners usually go? Do you have any traditions you'd like to share?**
4. This is the first time you hear from Serah's dad, aside from the prologue. What do you think about him?
5. **Serah's dad says, "Sometimes, the best is not the best. We need to choose our battles wisely." What do you think of that?**
6. Has your view of Serah's mom changed at all or stayed the same after learning more about her?
7. Who do you most relate to in Chapter 8 and why?
8. **Have you ever been a part of "mean girl" activity? If so, would you share the story? How did it**

make you feel? Do you know how it affected the others involved?

9. **Why do you think girls sometimes treat each other this way?**

10. Do you think Cecilia's stunt will have a good effect on her relationship with Josh or a bad one?

11. Do you think Serah purposely kicked the ball at Cecilia? Why or why not?

Homework: Send a positive message—either a handwritten note, a text, or a voicemail—to a person you're going through this study with in the next few days.

WEEK 5

1. Vittoria tells Serah that someday she will "do stupid things to get guys to like her." What do you think about that?

2. **What do you think would be appropriate things to do to "get a guy to like you"?**

3. **What are inappropriate things to do to "get a guy to like you"?**

4. After reading this chapter, do you feel differently about Vittoria? In what way(s)?

5. **Can you empathize with Vittoria? Why or why not?**

6. What has your family decided in terms of having an iPod, a cell phone, or other such device? What

are some of the benefits of these devices? What are some of the drawbacks?

7. Have you been bullied or tortured on your device, if you have one? Share the story if you're willing.

8. **Do you have any access to social media? What are the benefits of social media? What are the drawbacks?**

9. **Serah tells Mrs. Caldwell that sometimes she doesn't like the way her mom shows her that she cares. Mrs. Caldwell responds, "I don't know this for a fact, but I think every daughter has felt that way about her mother at some time or another." Would you agree or disagree with this statement? Why or why not?**

Homework: Take some time to think through things you don't want to do to get a crush to notice you. Write them down in a journal or diary so you can refer to them as you get older and hold yourself to your personal standards.

WEEK 6

1. Are there any things you absolutely wouldn't do to make yourself look beautiful? If so, what are they?

2. Have you been to an orthodontist, dermatologist, or any other doctor to help make your face look different? What do you think about these sorts of treatments?

3. **Serah asks her mother how she can believe she is beautiful "despite all her flaws." What would you say to her?**
4. **Can you be beautiful and smart? Is it easier for a guy to be handsome and smart than it is for a girl to be beautiful and smart?**
5. Are you harder or easier on yourself than you are on others? In what ways? Why do you think that is?
6. **Do you know anyone like Mandy King? How do you handle it? If we're honest, many of us have had at least a "Mandy King" moment, where we've treated others unkindly. How do you fix that after you've done it?**
7. **Where do our Mandy King moments come from?**
8. Does wearing a swimsuit seem embarrassing to you? Why or why not?
9. What about the swimming incident? Whose side would you take (if any)? Who can you relate to most—Serah, Jessica, or Liv? Why?

Homework: Think of some role models you know of who are both intelligent and beautiful. Bring the list with you next week.

WEEK 7

1. First, does anyone have some names of intelligent and beautiful women to share?

2. **What was your reaction to what happened to Serah? What do you think about how it affects her? What will it be like for her down the road?**

3. Do you have any visible scars that are noticeable? How did you get them? How do you feel about them?

4. **Serah assumed her mom misspelled her name, but she finds out she was wrong. Have you ever assumed something that hurt you, only to find out your assumption was wrong? How can we avoid doing this?**

5. Do you find it easier to believe the best about others or the worst? Would you say you're more of a skeptic or a positive person?

6. Do you have any family members you are close to, such as aunts, uncles, or grandparents? What role do they play in your life?

7. Have your parents ever kept something from you to protect you? How did you find out about it? And how did you feel when you found out? What about further down the road after time passed?

8. Have you ever been betrayed? Can you describe the feeling?

9. **On a scale from 1–10, how bad is the betrayal by Serah's parents and Mrs. Caldwell? How did you come to that conclusion?**
10. Should Serah forgive Seth? Why or why not?
11. How do you think Serah handled the Liv drama?

Homework: If you drew a picture of Serah after Week 1, draw a *new* color picture of Serah's face—without looking at your first one—based on what you think she looks like now. Be as detailed as possible. Bring it and your original drawing of Serah to the last group discussion. If you made a beautiful list instead, make sure it's up-to-date and bring it to the final discussion group.

WEEK 8

1. Is it okay that Serah's mom let Mrs. Caldwell in? Why or why not?
2. **What do you think of Mrs. Caldwell's story?**
3. Do you still believe she betrayed Serah? Why or why not?
4. **What do you think Serah did with her Beautiful List?**
5. **Do you think it's easier, harder, or no different to believe you are beautiful now than you did when you were three years old? Five? Seven? What about now compared to when you began reading this book?**

6. Do you have a dream that someone has told you is unreachable because of a limitation you have? Do you believe that person?

7. **What do you think it means to "live beautiful"?**

8. Are all girls beautiful?

9. **If you drew pictures of Serah, compare your drawings from before and after her accident. What do you notice? Is she more or less beautiful in one or the other? If you made a beautiful list, what have you added to it since you first made it?**

10. **What has Serah taught you? What about Rachel? Mrs. Caldwell? Mrs. Reynolds?**

11. **Share your main takeaway from the book.**

Homework: Share this book with someone who will enjoy it and review it on the site where you purchased it. If your parent or guardian is okay with it, snap a photo of you with the book and have your mom post it to her Meta (Facebook or Instagram) account and tag me:

Facebook - @ChristineEVirgin
Instagram - @christinevirgin

About the Author

Christine Elliott Virgin has been writing for years, but this is her first novel. She graduated from the University of North Carolina at Chapel Hill with a BA in journalism and mass communication as well as a minor in business administration. A former Charles Kuralt Fellow at Voice of America (VOA), her storytelling background comes  from both broadcast journalism and long-form documentary television production. Feeling called to make a difference in the lives of preteen and teenage girls, she quit her job in 2004 and co-launched *Realiteen*, a niche magazine that engaged pop culture from a Biblical worldview. After that venture failed, Christine landed in the production management department of Discovery Communications, where she earned credits on series such as *Man vs. Wild*, *Mythbusters*, Emmy-winning *Cash Cab*, and others.

In 2010, she started the blog peeinpeace.com as an outlet for both creativity and sanity as a stay-at-home mom with a toddler and an infant. Most recently, after having her third child in 2013, she spent three years as part-time web editor for the 21st Century Wilberforce Initiative, a global religious freedom non-profit in the DC area. The concept for *The Beautiful List* had been on her heart, but it took being in a cast for three months after ankle reconstruction surgery to finally put pen to paper.

Christine has published online articles in *Christianity Today* and *Today's Christian Woman*, as well as a devotional in a Proverbs 31 Ministries publication, *40 Reminders God is in Control: Devotions to Redirect Your Worry into Worship* (Fall 2020). She continues to blog at her author website, www.christinevirgin.com, where you can reach her because she is not famous and loves hearing from fans. She enjoys cooking and gardening and feels most alive when she drives cars as fast as she can on a racetrack. Christine resides outside Washington, DC, with her husband, three children, and quirky Australian labradoodle, Baxter.

A free ebook edition
is available with the
purchase of this book.

To claim your free ebook edition:

1. Visit MorganJamesBOGO.com
2. Sign your name CLEARLY in the space
3. Complete the form and submit a photo of
   the entire copyright page
4. You or your friend can download the ebook
   to your preferred device

Print & Digital Together Forever.

Snap a photo   Free ebook   Read anywhere

CPSIA information can be obtained
at www.ICGtesting.com
Printed in the USA
BVHW060956210322
631577BV00002B/11